lisa samson

Hollywood Nobody

Book 1

a novel

NAVPRESS

THINK

www.thinkbooks.com

TH1NK
P.O. Box 35001
Colorado Springs, Colorado 80935

TH1NK is an imprint of NavPress.
TH1NK and the TH1NK logo are registered trademarks of NavPress. Absence of ® in connection with marks of NavPress or other parties does not indicate an absence of registration of those marks.

ISBN-13: 978-1-60006-091-5
ISBN-10: 1-60006-091-9

Cover design by The DesignWorks Group, David Uttley, www.thedesignworksgroup.com
Cover image by Steve Gardner, www.shootpw.com
Creative Team: Erin Healy, Darla Hightower, Arvid Wallen, Kathy Guist

This novel is a work of fiction. Names, characters, places, and incidents are either the product of the author's imagination or are used fictitiously. Any resemblance to actual events, locales, organizations, or persons, living or dead, is entirely coincidental and beyond the intent of either the author or publisher.

Published in association with the literary agency of Alive Communications, Inc., 7680 Goddard Street, Suite 200, Colorado Springs, Colorado 80920 (www.alivecommunications.com).

Samson, Lisa, 1964-
  Hollywood nobody : a novel. Book 1 / Lisa Samson.
    p. cm.
  ISBN 978-1-60006-091-5
1. Parent and child--Fiction. 2. Teenage girls--Fiction. 3. Mothers and daughters--Fiction. 4. Single mothers--Fiction. 5. California--Fiction. 6. Christian fiction. 7. Domestic fiction. I. Title.
  PS3569.A46673H65 2007
  813'.54--dc22
                                2007015519

Printed in the United States of America

1 2 3 4 5 6 7 8 9 10 / 11 10 09 08 07

Other Young Adult Books by Lisa Samson

Apples of Gold

Dedication

for Jared
family

Acknowledgments

Thanks to all at NavPress who were a part of this: from those who began it all to those who brought it home.

To my daughter, Ty, who helped me with Scotty's voice and perspective. To Jared, King of YA fiction and in-house cheerleader.

Thanks to Jeanne Damoff for her much-appreciated "look-see" and for being Queen of Punctuation! To Erin Healy . . . as usual!

Thanks to all my family and friends who encouraged me. To Will, Jake, Gwynnie and Ty, especially.

And thanks to God for all things!

Hollywood Nobody: April 1

Happy April Fool's Day! What better day to start a blog about Hollywood than today?

Okay, I've been around film sets my whole life. Indie films, yeah, and that's all I'm saying about it here for anonymity's sake. But trust me, I've had my share of embarrassing moments. Like outgrowing Tom Cruise by the age of twelve — in more ways than one, with the way he's gotten crazier than thong underwear and low-rise jeans. Thankfully that fashion disaster has run for cover.

Underwear showing? Not a good idea.

Fact: I don't know of a single girl who doesn't wish the show-it-all boxer-shorts phenomenon would go away as well. Guys, we just don't want to see your underwear. Truthfully, we believe that there is a direct correlation between how much underwear you show and how much you've got upstairs, if you know what I mean.

I've seen the stars at their best and at their worst. And believe me, the worst is really, really bad. Big clue: you'd look just as pretty as they do if you went to such lengths. As you might guess, some of them are really nice and some of them are total jerks, and there's a lot of blah in-betweeners. Like real life, pretty much, only the extremes are more extreme sometimes. I mean honestly, how many people under twenty do *you* know who have had more than one plastic surgery?

So you'll have to forgive me if I'm a little hard on these folks. But if it was all sunshine and cheerleading, I doubt you'd read this blog for long, right?

Today's Rant: Straightening irons. We've had enough of them, Little Stars, okay? It was bad on Helen Hunt at the Oscars, worse on Demi, yet worse on Madonna, and it's still ridiculous.

Especially on those women who are trying to hold onto their youth like Gollum holds onto that ring. Ladies, there's a reason for keeping your hair at or above your shoulders once you hit forty, and ever after. Think Annette Bening. Now she's got it going on. And can't you just see why Warren Beatty settled down for her? Love her! According to *The Early Show* this morning, curls are back, and Little Me ain't going to tell why I'm so glad about that!

Today's Kudo: Aretha Franklin. Big, bold, beautiful, and the best. Her image is her excellence. Man, that woman can sing! She has a prayer chain too. I'm not very religious myself, but you got to respect people who back up what they say they believe. Unless it's male Scientologists and "silent birth." Yeah, right. Easy for them to say.

Today's News: I saw a young actor last summer at a Shakespeare festival in New England. Seth Haas. Seth Hot is more like it. I heard a rumor he's reading scripts for consideration. Yes, he's that hot. Check him out here. Tell all your friends about him. And look here on Hollywood Nobody for the first, the hottest news on this hottie. Girls, he's only nineteen! Fair game for at least a decade-and-a-half span of ages.

I don't know about you, but following the antics of new teen rock star Violette Dillinger is something I'm looking forward to. Her first album, released to much hype, hit Billboard's no. 12 spot its third week out. And don't you love her hit single "Love Comes Knocking on My Door"? This is going to be fun. A new celeb. Uncharted territory. Will Violette, who seems grounded and talented, be like her predecessors and fall into the "great defiling show-business machine" only to be spit out as a half-naked bimbo? We'll see, won't we? Keep your fingers crossed that the real artist survives.

Today's Quote: "Being thought of as 'a beautiful woman' has spared me nothing in life. No heartache, no trouble. Beauty is essentially meaningless." Halle Berry

Later!

Friday, April 2

I knew it was coming soon. We'd been camped out in the middle of a cornfield, mind you, for two weeks. That poke on my shoulder in the middle of the night means only one thing. Time to move on.

"What, Charley?"

"Let's head 'em on out, Scotty. We've got to be at a shoot in North Carolina tomorrow afternoon. I've got food to prepare, so you have to drive."

"I'm still only fifteen."

"It's okay. You're a good driver, baby."

My mom, Charley Dawn, doesn't understand that laws exist for a reason, say, keeping large vehicles out of the hands of *children*. But as a food stylist, she fakes things all the time.

Her boundaries are blurred. What can I say?

Charley looks like she succumbed to the peer pressure of plastic surgery, but she hasn't. I know this because I'm with her almost all the time. I think it's the bleached-blond fountain of long hair she's worn ever since I can remember. Or maybe the hand-dyed sarongs and shirts from Africa, India, or Bangladesh add to the overall appearance of youth. I have no idea. But it really makes me mad when anybody mistakes us as sisters.

I mean, come on! She had me when she was forty!

My theory: a lot of people are running around with bad eye-sight and just don't know it.

I throw the covers to my left. If I sling them to my right, they'd land on the dinette in our "home," to use the term in a fashion less meaningful than a Hollywood "I do." I grew up in this old Travco RV I call the Y.

As in Y do I have to live in this mobile home?

Y do I have to have such an oddball food stylist for a mother?

Y must we travel all year long? Y will we never live anyplace long enough for me to go to the real Y and take aerobics, yoga, Pilates or—shoot—run around the track for a while, maybe swim laps in the pool?

And Y oh Y must Charley be a vegan?

More on that later.

And Y do I know more about Hollywood than I should, or even want to? Everybody's an actor in Hollywood, and I mean that literally. Sometimes I wonder if any of them even know who they are deep down in that corner room nobody else is allowed into. But I wonder the same thing about myself.

"You're not asking me to drive while you're in the kitchen trailer, are you, Charley?"

"No. I can cook in here. And it's a pretty flat drive. I'll be fine."

I'm not actually worried about her. I'm thinking about how many charges the cops can slap on me.

Driving without a license.

Driving without a seat belt on the passenger.

Speeding, because knowing Charley, we're late already.

Driving without registration. Charley figured out years ago how to lift current stickers off of license plates. She loves "sticking it to the man." Or so she says.

I kid you not.

Oh, the travails of a teenager with an old hippie for a mother. Charley is oblivious as usual as I continue my recollection of past infractions thankfully undetected by the state troopers:

Driving while someone's in the trailer. It's a great trailer, don't get me wrong, a mini industrial kitchen we rigged up a couple of years ago to make her job easier. Six-range burner, A/C, and an exhaust fan that sucks up more air than Joan Rivers schmoozing on the red carpet. But it's illegal for her to go cooking while we're in motion.

"All right. Can I at least get dressed?"

"Why? You're always in your pj's anyway."

"Great, Mom."

"It's Charley, baby. You know how I feel about social hierarchy."

"But didn't you just give me an order to drive without a license? What if I say no?"

She reaches into the kitchen cupboard without comment and tips down a bottle of cooking oil. Charley's as tall as a twelve-year-old.

"I mean, let's be real, *Charley*. You do, in the ultimate end of things, call the shots."

I reach back for my glasses on the small shelf I installed in the side of the loft. It holds whatever book I'm reading and my journal. I love my glasses, horn-rimmed "cat glasses" as Charley calls them. Vintage 1961. Makes me want to do the twist and wear penny loafers.

"Can I at least pull my hair back?"

She huffs. "Oh, all right, Scotty! Why do you have to be so difficult?"

Charley has no clue as to how difficult teenagers can actually be. Here I am, schooling myself on the road, no wild friends. No friends at all, actually, because I hate Internet friendships. I mean, how lame, right? No boyfriend, no drugs. No alcohol either, unless you count cold syrup, because the Y gets so cold during the winter and Charley's a huge conservationist. (Big surprise there.) I should be thankful, though. At least she stopped wearing leather fringe a couple of years ago.

I slide down from the loft, gather my circus hair into a ponytail, and slip into the driver's seat. Charley reupholstered it last year with rainbow fabric. I asked her where the unicorns were and she just rolled her eyes. "Okay, let's go. How long is it going to take?"

"Oh." She looks down, picks up a red pepper and hides behind it.

I turn on her. "You didn't Google Map it?"

"You're the computer person, not me." She peers above the stem. "I'm sorry?" She shrugs. Man, I hate it when she's so cute. "Really sorry?"

"Charley, we're in Wilmore, Kentucky. As in Ken-Tuck-EEE. As in the middle of nowhere." I climb out of my seat. "What part of North Carolina are we going to? It's a wide state."

"Toledo Island. Something like that. Near Ocracoke Island. Does that sound familiar?"

"The Outer Banks?"

"Are they in North Carolina?"

Are you kidding me?

"Let me log on. This is crazy, Charley. I don't know why you do this to me all the time."

"Sorry." She says it so Valley Girl-like. I really thought I'd be above TME: Teenage Mom Embarrassment. But no. Now, most kids don't have mothers who dress like Stevie Nicks and took a little too much LSD back in the DAY. It doesn't take ESP to realize who the adult in this setup is. And she had me, PDQ, out of the bonds of holy matrimony I might add, when she was forty (yes, I already told you that, but it's still just as true), and that's OLD to be caught in such an inconvenient situation, don't you think? The woman had no excuse for such behavior, FYI.

My theory: Charley's a widow and it's too painful to talk about my father. I mean, it's plausible, right?

The problem is, I can remember back to when I was at least four, and I definitely do not remember a man in the picture. Except for Jeremy. More on him later too.

I flip up my laptop. I have a great satellite Internet setup in the Y. I rigged it myself because I'm a lonely geek with nothing better to do with her time than figure out this kind of stuff. I type in the info and wait for the directions. Satellite is slower than DSL, but it's better than nothing.

"Charley! It's seventeen hours away!" I scan the list of twists and turns between here and there. "We have to take a ferry to Ocracoke, and then Toledo Island's off of there."

"Groovy!"

"*Groovy* died with platform shoes and midis."

"Whatever, Scotty." Only she says it all sunny. She's a morning person.

"That phrase *should* be dead."

Honestly, I'm not big on lingo. I've never been good at it,

which is fine by me. Who am I going to impress with cool-speak anyway? Uma Thurman? Yeah, right. "Okay, let's go."

"We can go as long as possible and break camp on the way, you know?" Charley.

I climb back into the rainbow chair, throw the Y into drive, pull the brake, and we're moving on down the road.

Again.

Eight hours later

On the road since well before daylight, I hear my stomach suggest lunch. We've wound our way through Kentucky, chopping off a corner of Virginia, and buzzed into North Carolina. No way am I pushing the speed. No way. Charley is crazy if she thinks I'm going to do that. We'll be fine at this pace, but I don't want Charley to know it. She can sweat it out a little. Maybe we'll leave a day earlier next time. And Wilmore, Kentucky? Are you kidding me? Who'd want to stay there any longer than necessary?

Are all mothers so high-maintenance, so in need of instruction?

"Are we going to have lunch?"

Charley glances up from the range, where she chars red peppers. Don't worry. The windows are open and I installed a range hood last year. "Oh, right! I forgot. Let's see what we've got. Will a sandwich be okay?"

"Yeah. I can keep driving."

Charley makes good sandwiches. She's vegan, but somehow

she knows what to do with sauces. But what I'd do for a piece of cheese on those veggie pitas leads me to suspect that moral failure really is just around the corner for most people and for the smallest of reasons.

She pushes a lock of long silver-blond hair from her tired eyes.

"I could just do fast food."

She nods. "I'm so behind, you know? Can you do Subway or something? You can get a veggie sub there. Here's an apple for now."

Charley's voice is soft and musical.

Okay. Another hour down the road, a highway sign advertises a Subway at the next exit. And KFC (love Original Recipe), Long John Silvers (Chicken Planks and Fish Fillets!) and Biscuitville (Sausage Biscuits . . . with Cheese!). Must be some strange town without a McDonald's or a Burger King, but who am I to question? I pull into the lot. "I'll be right back."

She hands me a ten. "I'll stay here. Remember, veggie subs, baby. Don't think I won't smell the meat. You know I'm like a raccoon when it comes to animal product."

Oh joy! I practically skip inside. On my own. The Vegan Sheriff behind me in the camper.

I explain my dilemma to the sub maker, a lady anybody in their right mind would want as their grandmother.

"Sure, I'll bury the cheese, honey."

"And put a star or something on the wrapper so I know which is mine, okay?"

"All right. Want that heated up so it's all melted and good?"

"Definitely."

"It's less likely to fall out too. We simply can't have that."

My partner in crime!

"True. Thanks."

Her wink settles on my face like a kiss.

Back on the road, I loll in dairy Nirvana. Man, I love cheese. My one rebellion. Pretty sad, huh?

Charley sits at the dinette, talking to me as she consumes her sandwich like a mountain climber who has been lost in the Andes without food for a week. I suspect that vegans are always hungry. I eat while I drive, as much to hide the provolone, Swiss, cheddar, pepper jack and white American as I do to make time. "So hey, what kind of movie is it? Who's directing?"

"It's a smart romantic comedy and it's Jeremy's picture."

"That's nice."

So here's the scoop on Jeremy: Charley works on all of Jeremy Winger's films. They were friends back in the early seventies in some artsy commune or something. Charley used to be a great artist, I've heard. How much pot they smoked between the two of them is anybody's guess. But as far as I know, he's as clean as my mother now. Just as weird, though. But I like him. A lot. Jeremy feels responsible for me for some reason, but I don't think he's my father even if we do both have pale skin and hitchhiker's thumbs.

"Have you read the script?"

"Just the scenes I need to. It's a Southern-type thing. Lots of fried chicken, tomatoes, okra and stuff."

"What's it about?"

"A young couple just out of high school. He's a working-class guy and she's from an upper-crust family."

"Oooh, how original."

"I think there's a kind of twist, though. Jeremy wouldn't be doing it if it was cliché."

True. Like maybe the girl has a wasting disease and the boy hates his feet so much he goes on a hunger strike.

"And lots of party scenes in there too. I think it's a modern retelling of *The Great Gatsby*. But more Southern, homespun. And the characters are at a younger place in life."

"Are you kidding me? *The Great Gatsby* is my favorite book!"

As if I have to tell her that. My full name is Frances Scott Fitzgerald Dawn. Just like F. Scott Fitzgerald who wrote *The Great Gatsby* in the first place. Only he's Francis. The boy spelling. Charley doesn't say much about Fitzgerald at all really, and I don't think she's ever read any of his works. When I asked her about it once she said, "I just thought the name sounded groovy."

My theory: I'm named after my father.

"Who are the mains?"

"Some young star named Karissa something."

"Karissa Bonano?"

"I think."

Oh wow. "She's a good actress. Wild, though, and she had the freakiest boob job last year. But still, I can totally picture her as ditz-head Daisy. Who else?"

"Seth House?"

"Seth Haas?"

"I guess."

"Seth Haas?! I love him!" I dragged Jeremy to a play Seth was in last summer so he could see the guy in action.

"Really? Far out."

"You don't remember when we saw him in Connecticut a couple of years ago?"

"Honestly, baby, all those young guys tend to blend together, you know?"

Seth Haas as a young Jay Gatsby. Well, he's not at all like Robert Redford, who played Jay Gatsby a century ago, but he could pull off a bit of mystery. He really could.

And man, is he gorgeous.

All right, then, let's get this Y to Toledo Island! This might not be the drag I thought.

Later

Love Child: Breaker 1 – 9. Breaker 1 – 9. This is Love Child. Anybody copy?

Maverick: Maverick here. I gotta copy, c'mon.

Love Child: I'm heading east on I-40. Where are you?

Maverick: Heading west at the 200-mile marker, c'mon.

Love Child: Copy that, Maverick. I'm looking for anybody in an RV headed toward Cape Hatteras, copy?

Maverick: That ain't me, but good luck, Love Child.

Grampie: Breaker 1 – 9 to the Love Child. Come in, Love Child.

Love Child: This is Love Child, you gotta copy.

Grampie: This is Grampie.

Love Child: Copy that, Grampie! Let's take it down to channel eleven, copy?

Grampie: Copy that, amigo. See you there.

I switch the channel on my CB radio. I love the crazy gadget. Charley bought it for me on my twelfth birthday. "You gotta have some sorta fun on the road, Scotty." And I've met all sorts of cool people. She's had some second thoughts, believe me. I don't think she realized how likeable I can actually be.

And Grampie! He's my favorite older man on the road. Bob comes in at a close second. And Grammie! She's the best lady in the world. Doris doesn't even come close, but that's just because Grammie's so great in a really unusual way, wearing turbans and gold jewelry and sparkly shoes. Grammie and Grampie are like fun teenagers with all the responsibility and love of people who've been down the road a time or two.

Grampie: Breaker 1 – 1, Grampie lookin' for Love Child.

Love Child: I gotta copy, Grampie.

Grampie: How you doin', amigo?

Love Child: Great! Just saw me some bear bait flying by. Better him than me! Are you heading toward Cape Hatteras?

Grampie: We are. We'll be at the KOA there. We'll be getting in around suppertime.

Love Child: Us too.

Grampie: I'll tell Grammie to put on some extra chops. I'll sneak one to you after your mother goes to bed.

Love Child: I can't wait.

Grampie: It'll be good to see you again, honey. It's been a while. Too long.

Love Child: Yeah, Grampie. Way too long. Tell Grammie I can't wait to see her too.

Grampie: Will do!

A minute later

Charley emerges from the rest stop's bathroom, talking on her cell phone. Worry rains down over her face. I climb out of the cab and she turns her back on me, hunched over the secret conversation. She's had these clandestine exchanges for the past three or four years.

I've learned not to ask her about them. She may be ditzy and sweet, but not about those phone calls. Sometimes you just know where somebody's built her fences.

An RV pulls up beside ours, silver and sleek, a converted Blue Bird bus, custom, and what a beaut! Across the side, the words *Happy Couple* in classy script announce exactly who is inside.

The door opens with an airy punch and out steps Doris, then Bob.

"Scotty!" Doris cries, her hands waving just below the cuffs of her long, yellow cracker-barrel sleeves. Three birdhouse appliqués perch on her Aretha-sized chest. Her poodle curls, obviously benefiting from a brown drugstore rinse, shuffle in the Carolina breeze.

"Group hug!" Bob spreads wide his plaid flannel-wrapped arms.

They fold me into their embrace like chocolate chips into pancake batter. They smell so much like regular people. No exotic spices or natural fibers. I breathe deeply, hoping to take a few particles of normal inside my lungs.

When we pull apart, Doris squeezes my arm and smiles at me with fake white teeth. "I'm so glad you haven't pulled out yet. I told Bob that was your RV, so we went down to the next exit and turned around. I thought, 'Oh, my! We're never going to make it,' and here you still are!"

"Most definitely! How are you guys?"

They fill me in on their travels in the three months since we saw each other in Florida. Visited two of their seven kids and loads of grandkids. Had a lovely Valentine's for two on Key West. And despite a breakdown in Mississippi, it's been a good winter. They met the nicest family in Mississippi and oh, there are good folks everywhere, aren't there, Scotty?

What a life! Doris and Bob just plain know how live.

"Where are you headed?" Bob takes a knee to check the air pressure in a tire.

"Cape Hatteras tonight. I'm meeting up with Billie Jo and George at the KOA, then we're headed onto Ocracoke Island for a little while." I knew better than to say *Toledo Island* with the way Charley is so jumpy about everything. Even offering up Ocracoke is taking a crazy chance.

Doris gasps. "You don't say! Oh, Bob, isn't that a coincidence?"

"Why? You guys going there?"

"No, dear. We're heading out to California for my grandson's graduation. But my niece lives on Ocracoke. Her name's Joy Overstreet and she works at a little diner there."

"Really?"

"What's it called? The Ten Clams, I think. It's a small community. Please give her our regards, won't you?"

"Sure. Is she nice?"

"You bet." Bob stands up. Tires are all good I guess. "I hear she's having a rough time making ends meet. Off-season can be pretty hard."

Doris nods. "She could probably use a friendly visitor about now."

Charley comes running around the RV. "Let's go."

"Charley, it's Bob and Doris!"

"Hi, guys." She lays a hand on my arm. "I said let's go."

"Okay. I'll be there in a minute."

"Now!" She hops in the Y.

I offer Bob and Doris a pseudo-pout as an apology. "Gotta go." I open my door. "See you guys later!"

Doris knits her brows. "A-all right. Good-bye, honey. Nice seeing you."

"'Bye, Scotty! Take care now." Bob.

I start the van. "You're crazy, Charley, you know that. That was so rude."

"Just drive, Scotty. Get us out of here. Take the side roads for a while."

I pull out and grab for the map I picked up at the rest area. Great. It will be midnight before we pull in, I just know it.

"Did you tell them where we're going?"

Shoot. Why is she asking that? "No. I didn't say a word."

"Good girl."

I hate it when I lie to her. I hate it so much.

Hours later

Just after eight o'clock, we pull into the Cape Hatteras KOA. Man, those beachside parks really stiff us with their prices. We could have stayed in a hotel, had a normal shower where you don't have to scrape the curtain off your wet body to get out, maybe enjoyed a little continental breakfast in the lobby, but no. Charley never wants to have fun like that. She always claims we can make our fun between the two of us. But if that's happening, well, she must be the one having all the fun.

I hop out of the Y, stretch my back. Grammie and Grampie are already waiting outside their RV, sitting in camp chairs, his hand resting on her leg, hers on his. Grammie sometimes wears bright green high heels. Grampie sometimes smokes a pipe.

Tonight they do both.

They don't see me yet. They chat and I can imagine their conversation about old-people's rights or the state of the arts these days.

Grammie looks like she used to be a model back in the day but settled into the role of a slightly overweight Food Network cooking goddess. Grampie's just a distinguished-looking older man who writes travel articles for magazines like *AARP* and *TrailerLife*. You should see the meals they dream up in the kitchen of their RV. In their case, it almost seems disrespectful to use the term *RV*. This is Buckingham Palace on wheels. A Beaver Marquis. Now what I wouldn't give to motor through Charley's crazy schedule in one of those babies! Built just for you. Half a million dollars a pop.

Crazy talk!

They are *so* loaded.

"Scotty!" They stand.

Grammie, aka Billie Jo, wraps me in her tanned arms sprinkled with age spots ranging from caramel to dark chocolate. I can't see the spots because she's wearing a jacket, but I know they're hiding under there. "Oh, Lovie! George said he'd made contact with you. Come on in! Where's your mother? I was hoping to finally meet her this time."

I first met Grammie and Grampie about a year ago. "She's gone to bed already. I pulled in on my own."

"Yes, well, you know the drill by now." George.

"Most definitely."

He embraces me too. And I smell Unique pipe tobacco and shaving lotion.

Every time I ascend into their RV, I want to gasp. Burled-wood cabinetry and tables polished to a gleaming sheen. Cream-colored leather upholstery, brass fittings. Hardwood floors and plush carpets. Yeah, easy to see why they chose the road, these two. No compromise here. Not to mention they both confess to their wanderlust. "We don't have any children, so why not? We're in great shape, so why place limitations on ourselves?" Grammie told me this when we first met. "Plus, we can write it off on our taxes. Research you know." She is also a writer. Poetry and drug-store romances under a pseudonym. She said she wouldn't give me one until I turn sixteen.

Her poetry makes me feel like I could soar over a rainforest, or the pyramids, if that's what I wanted to do.

"Glad you're here!" George hugs me, then leads me into their RV. George Roberts Wethington, and if that isn't a name you'd only expect to find in the stereotypical world of screen writing, I don't know what is. He isn't snooty, though, and he earned every dime of his retirement fund by manufacturing pantyhose. I kid you not. "Let me get out your plate."

"Sorry it took me longer."

"It always takes longer than you think." Grammie, born Billie Jo Katherine Moriarty, lays out some silverware. Nice stuff, of course.

"What did you make?"

"A mixed grill!" Grampie turns with the plate. Now *he* should be a movie star. His thick white hair grows back from his forehead like a mane. He wears starched button-downs. He seems to smile even when his face is relaxed. "Salmon, chicken breast, and a filet mignon."

"Can I just die right now?" I ask.

"Not until you eat every bite. I didn't slave over a hot stove so you could go belly up." Grampie sets down the plate. "Organic and cruelty-free too."

"Don't ruin it for me. You're starting to sound like Charley."

They both sit with me, looking as if every word I'm about to say will be the best thing they've ever heard. They look so cute side by side.

Charley doesn't think I have family besides her. But she's dead wrong about that.

"Love your new glasses!" Grammie says. "They're the real deal, aren't they?"

And Grammie should know, having a lot in common with real deals.

Two hours later

Still. I punch my pillow, lay my head down, then pull back the curtain to gaze at the stars. I'd give up a lot to know what it's like to live a real life, even for just a month. I wish I could rely on Charley to be the consistent, soft, and safe mom that a lot of kids have. But she's sad. And always running away. You can only get so close to someone that frightened of life.

Give me a month in a real house with a mom who yells at me for not doing my homework or gets exasperated because she actually notices I forget to brush my hair. Give me a dad who's disappointed in a C in biology because he knows I could make A's or even better, who scoops up ice cream in a mug and invites me to sit on the sofa and watch *Law & Order*. Strike that—I haven't enjoyed that one since Benjamin Bratt left. What a hottie, and was Julia Roberts temporarily insane?

I possess almost all the freedom a girl could have. All the freedom and no place to go, no place to just be.

Dear Elaine,

It's been a while since I've written in your pages and I cringe at the thought of our visits. Writing in a diary is so . . . I don't know . . . typical, I guess. But it makes me feel normal when I do it, connected somehow to all the other teenagers who write in diaries even if they don't live on the road in a really old, crappy RV. When I pick up my pen, I feel a sort of ethereal connection. Like I am one of them. Of course, I know I'm not. I'm nothing like them with their pretty lives, straightening my pretty hair, going to my pretty school, eating my pretty dinner, walking next door to my pretty friend's house to watch pretty people on TV. Coming home and showering before sliding into my pretty bed.

That's another thing: Charley hates using up water. I have to literally sneak my showers if I want one every day. The days she doesn't leave the Y, I'm forced to use her biodegradable, chemical-free baby wipes.

So, Elaine. Here we go again. I saw this teenage girl tonight sitting around the campfire with her dad. And she was so mad at him she looked like flames were going to start sparking from the ends of her hair and out of her nostrils. Yeah, she had used a straightening iron too. Argh!!

The dad tried to put his arm around her and she did this shruggy little wiggle, got up, and walked away with her arms folded so tightly around her middle I'm surprised she could breathe. Even if she could have seen how sad his eyes were, I doubt it would have mattered.

I wonder where my dad is? Who he is? I wonder that you haven't banned me from asking the same questions over and over. I'll never ask Charley about it again. I don't think she even knows the answer. That's kinda gross, if you ask me. Yuck. I hate seeing her as this slutty girl and try not to think about it in front of her. But I'm so different from her! She doesn't begin to understand me, and her being so hippie-like hasn't done one bit to help her see things from my point of view. I'm not stupid enough to think that my father, beyond a shadow of a doubt, would either. But I sure like to think he might.

I like to cook. Does he like to cook?

I love computers. Does he?

I love Sylvia Plath. Does he? Well, probably not, but there's no harm in pretending. And it's not like she's my absolute favorite anyway.

I'll bet he's totally in love with cheese like I am. I mean, that is something you just can't take credit for all on your own.

I miss him. I miss a man I've never met. That's really lame, isn't it?

Hollywood Nobody: April 2, 11:45 p.m.

Hey there, all you Nobodies. Believe me, if you're not in Hollywood right now, you are one. They're so darn cliquish on the West Coast of fantasyland. They're people who've finally made it to the popular crowd, who relish being *it* so much they'll do anything to retain their "it-ishness." I don't blame them really. A lot of actors and actresses were the <u>drama nerds</u> in high school, and you can still see the residual truth around the edges, despite the surgical enhancements, the makeup, the toned bodies, and the money. The prime example? When Leonardo DiCaprio runs. It's the nerdiest thing I've ever seen. Honestly, if they think we don't see what's going on, they must be nuts. And why a lot of them don't realize we'd like them perfectly well for who they really are mystifies me. I mean, everybody loves <u>Joan Cusack</u>, right? Today's Rant finished. Onto—

Today's Quote and Kudo: And oh my goodness! <u>Scarlett Johansson</u> loves cheese! "My greatest vice is cheese. Nothing else reigns over my life." She said in the *Observer*, a UK paper. Now, she shows "her girls" off like an elementary-school boy shows off whatever Japanimation cards are cool right now, but I'll forgive her for all that if she loves cheese. And besides, the girl isn't starving herself, and I love that about her.

Today's News: <u>Annette Bening</u> is purported to be the grande dame star at the shoot I'll be on tomorrow. Can't tell you where it is until we've hit the road and are long gone, folks. But stay tuned for more news on the star I dub "No. 1 Least Pathetic."

Remember, this is the place to find out all you can on <u>Seth</u>

<u>Haas,</u> because that's what I'll be doing! Basic stats:

Age: 19 (20 in July!)

Place of Birth: Washington, DC

Graduated From: NYU and yes he's übersmart

Height: 6'2"

Weight: 190

Eyes: Gray

Hair: Dark brown, wavy

Orientation: Straight

More on Seth Haas tomorrow. Will I get to meet him? Who knows?

Comments:

Great blog! Just found you today. I'll check out Seth Haas. I'm linking to you on my blog. — hollywoodjunkie, 8:29 a.m.

Scarlett Johansson is my fave new star. I say she should show off her girls all she likes. Flaunt it if you've got it! — GirlsGirls-Girls, 9:02 a.m.

I'll bet you run worse than Leo does. Give the guy a break! — titanicfan, 10:55 a.m.

Thanks everybody! Please link to me so we can get the word out! — hnobody, 1:00 p.m.

Saturday, April 3

I kissed Grammie and Grampie early in the morning, then delivered the Y to the ferry for Ocracoke in plenty of time. I'm a good planner. Charley says she doesn't know what she would do half the time without me. I just got so sick and tired of being late everywhere we went, I decided to take matters into my own hands. But I don't tell her that. Charley's one of those sweet people you really don't want to hurt unless it's absolutely necessary. I know she seems a little crotchety, but she's under a lot of pressure, what with starting a new film and harboring all of her secrets.

It's not a two-hour ferry ride, it's a forty-minute ferry ride. Those Internet map services are like people who leave an hour early to make a thirty-mile drive. I should know better than to trust their timing.

I stand on the forward deck, right by the bow slicing through the blue-gray waters of Pamlico Sound, Atlantic Ocean rolling to my left, all this blue, all this deep, all around this little boat—little in comparison to the waters—and I'm reminded even more of how small my life really is. Just a girl in a camper. So I head back to the Y, pull out my hot-pink soccer-mom chair, fire up the satellite Internet and begin to search for info on Ocracoke Island. I do become a sort of local historian on location. Usually there's nothing else to do. Charley specializes in offbeat places with offbeat directors. I'd love to say we head to glamorous locations studded by people in silk sarongs, necks strangled with diamonds and gold—or shoot—just Lilly Pulitzer purses hanging on their arms, but normally we stick to the backwater places where production costs are low.

She said they're shooting quite a bit of the movie here. It's pretty low-budget. I think Bening's doing it because she likes the script and working with Jeremy. He's really a well-respected director. And he's nice. I've known him all my life and he never forgets my birthday. I guess he's a little daddish to me. Too bad he's not Grammie and Grampie's son. That would tie my little fantasy family together neatly.

Ocracoke Island, NC. An easy Google and cool! There'll be some fun stuff to do. Blackbeard the pirate was killed here. Wow. Piratey stuff. I'm going to check that out.

A deserted town too. Plymouth. You can take a tour over there. Okay, check. And finally, Toledo Island. Very, very cute. They bill it as "A Step Back in Time." Apparently there's an active community council that oversees new building projects and doesn't allow commercialism to take over the beaches. There are two old hotels and a restored fishing village that, I'm sure, will be swarming with cast and crewmembers.

This'll all make up a good unit for me in history.

Is there a college in the world that's going to take a chance on my hodgepodge of learning? Some kids are homeschooled. I'm roadschooled. And I do it all by myself. I've never taken a standardized test because Charley won't allow it. I had to sign up for my satellite Internet service under a falsified age. Another lie to Charley, who thinks it's free. Little does she know I have my own credit card that I pay off by money order every month. She does give me a great allowance, I have to say, and I save most of it, because someday, I'm going to go to college and get out of this old tin can of a home.

We're puttering into the harbor of Ocracoke. Oh wow. Is this place quaint or what? Now to some, quaint equals boring. Not me. In these places real life is lived, not like what you find in Hollywood movies. I need these places to survive like I need air. And cheese.

Thirty minutes later, we cross the bridge onto Toledo Island and my heart sinks. It's so beautiful I'll never want to leave. And I'll have to. Why couldn't Jeremy have done another one of his edgy movies about poverty or addiction?

Three hours later

We're set up right on location now. Charley's got the kitchen trailer going full speed, frying chicken and blanching corn on the cob for the scene this morning, something taking place at a big party. It's Gatsby, right? But set in the South during the Depression, it includes some great party scenes. They'll need ice-cream cones as well.

So get this: most of the ice-cream cones used for photo shoots and movies are actually mashed potatoes. For one, they don't melt, for two, they scoop out in that perfect form. Want chocolate chips? Let me shave up a brown crayon! Pretty yucky though, right? These'll be strawberry, so she's working on getting that perfect shade of pink.

I should probably find Joy Overstreet and give her Bob and Doris's message. Firing up the Internet once again, I Google her name. *Whoa.* A lot more than an address in Ocracoke pops up.

According to the article, she used to be a fashion designer, but disappeared from the scene a couple of years ago just when she was on the brink of übersuccess.

Are you kidding me?

And here I thought I'd get to spend time with somebody normal. Of course, if anyone can define "normal" for me, I'll give them a fabulous parting gift.

Sunday, April 4

I pull my scooter from the underneath storage area of the Y. It's motorized, has a little seat, and makes me look like a total loser because Charley insists I wear a helmet. She cares, she cares. Oh, well. I strap on the black helmet I decorated with adhesive gems in the shape of a fifties-looking cat with huge eyes. I've always had an affinity for cats, and we really could have one in the Y, but Charley says no. She is slightly allergic to them, and the litter pan would smell in such limited space. Then there's the minor fact that the poor thing would be so confined, and if we let it out while we were parked somewhere, it might never come back. But still.

Off I go, zipping away from location, skirting equipment and cables, down to the village. Sunday mornings are my favorite time of the week, and for some reason they always have been. I like to ride by churches and hear the singing, watch people emerge, chat with each other, get in their cars and zip off for Sunday dinner at Denny's or somewhere.

I'm not disappointed along that line today. I slow down, then stop in front of Toledo Island Holy Spirit Church. The singing is loud and old-school. "Power, power, wonder working power. In the blood of the Lamb."

Christians seem to like lambs a lot, I've noticed. I'm not really up on Christianity, but any idiot has heard that Jesus is the Lamb of God, right?

A vinyl banner stretches between two posts stuck into the turf of the church yard.

APRIL 18–23

Tent Meeting

with

Hank and Kim Jones, Evangelists

"Be Blessed. Be Very Blessed."

Except for that ridiculous movie-trailer bit at the end, it sounds intriguing. Are they really going to set up a tent? I need to find out more about this sort of thing.

I'll explore the island later. We'll be here for a month according to Charley. Of course, that could change at a moment's notice.

Later

Charley's exhausted, so I fix her a grilled tofu-and-spinach sandwich with my own mix of spices. I swear, you've got to perfect the right seasonings to even begin eating this way.

I wasted so much time researching tent meetings today I blew off school, so I've got to catch up on my reading. I decided to do a unit on F. Scott Fitzgerald, who was really a pretty cool guy. So

I'm going to make up a thermos of coffee, grab a flashlight and a blanket, then head out to the beach once she's asleep.

She bites into the sandwich. "This is great. You sure have a way with food, baby."

"Thanks." I bite into my own. What I wouldn't give for a crappy old grilled Velveeta right now. Oh, man, now I'm going to be craving cheese. Is Velveeta technically cheese, though? "So it was a tiring day?"

"Uh-huh. Tomorrow's more of the same."

"What time do you have to get up?"

"Four."

"Yikes. You'd better go right to bed."

"Oh, I will." She looks up and smiles. Charley's smile speeds up your heart. "You doing okay, Scotty?"

"Sure. It's a neat little island."

"Groovy. But don't wander too far. Stick to the set and town where there's lots of people. No going on the beach alone." She reaches out and takes my hand. "You're a good kid, baby. I can't imagine life without *you*."

I pour a glass of soy milk and set it in front of her.

Despite all of my complaining, I really love Charley. How could I not?

She heads to the bed in the back of the camper, and by the time I've done the dishes, she's snoring like an old lady.

Coffee brewed and in the thermos, I grab my backpack and head out, not firing up the scooter until I'm far enough away for Charley not to hear.

I feel bad for sneaking out like this, going to the beach when she just told me not to, but if I lived the life Charley needed me to live, I'd practically be on a leash, unable to wander more than twenty feet from the Y. Like I say, she could have it a lot worse. I could be acting all like Lindsay Lohan and Tara Reid. Charley's thankful. I mean, she's seen those girls, and it's because she digs in her heels over stuff like this, I know there's a lot she's not telling me. And it's big stuff. Why else would we be flying under the radar, cash only, don't tell a soul, every single day of our lives?

What did she do that's so bad?

The beaches here on Toledo possess a gauzy remoteness because nobody's allowed to build on the oceanfront. I rest my scooter against a thick outgrowth of sea oats and navigate the boardwalk pathway between the dunes.

Oh my gosh!

Little ghosts look like they're dancing across the sand. I reach into my backpack, pull out the flashlight, and shine it across the beach. Tiny white sand crabs scurry around with their funny sideways gait. They're so cute!

Yeah, I know. They're crabs. But they're so cute!

Hey, I'll take whatever company I can get.

I spread out the blanket, lie down, rest the flashlight against my shoulder, and lift up old F. Scott. He sure had his ups and downs despite famous friends like Hemingway, Gertrude Stein, and T. S. Eliot, to name a few. They all lived in Paris for a while, met at bars and cafes. Completely artsy. Truly cool. And they had each other, at least on a very basic level.

They called themselves the Lost Generation. Imagine being part of a bona fide group with its own name.

Soon I'm enmeshed on Long Island in the roaring twenties and—can I be honest?—I'm not sure what Gatsby sees in Daisy to get all obsessed about her. But hey, who am I to judge? That line, "They say he killed a man once" sets my mind on a roller coaster.

After a while, my eyelids feel like they've gained ten pounds. Time for the coffee. So I sit up, unscrew the thermos, and pour some into the cup.

"Is that coffee I smell?"

The voice shoots out of the dark.

"Yeah. Who is that?"

"I'm over here. I just came for a walk on the beach and I saw you reading and didn't want to disturb you so I just sat and looked at all the critters instead."

What a run-on sentence!

He stands in front of me now, against the starlight, his outline dark, but somehow friendly the way his hands are shoved in his pockets and he puts his weight on his right leg, a little hunched.

I hold up the thermos. "Want some?"

"That would be great."

"Have a seat."

Okay, right. Alarm bells are going off, but not too loud. I'd love a little real conversation. And he's young. Not as young as me, I think. But not as old as Charley either.

I pour the coffee into the plastic cup and hand it to him.

"Are you sure?" he says. "What'll you drink out of?"

"I'll just sip from the thermos."

"Okay, if you're sure." He sips. "Nice. So are you from the island?"

Which pretty much tells me he's not.

"No. My mom's working on the movie shoot."

"Yeah? What's she do?"

"She's the food stylist."

"Very cool."

"Are you here for the shoot?"

"Yeah. It's crazy over there."

"Which is why I'm over here."

"Smart girl."

I sip too and hey, it is pretty good. I learned how to roast my own beans last year. That was actually something Charley encouraged. "I've been on more shoots than I can count. Like anything else, it gets old."

"Oh yeah? How so?"

I cross my legs semi yoga-style. "Well, it reminds me of an old men's club in some big city. All these old guys sitting around reading the newspaper and thinking they're so cool. Well, if they're so cool, why are they stuck in such a ghetto, you know?"

"You think the film industry is a ghetto?"

"Big time. But you probably have to be an inside-outsider to really see it. I'll tell you one thing: there's no way I'm going to go near Hollywood when I grow up." And could I be blabbering anymore than this? Good grief, Scotty, shut up, why don't you?

"How old are you?"

"Fifteen. Sixteen in June. June sixth. D-day." That was geeky.

"Have you ever been to Normandy?"

"No, have you?"

"Yeah. I went there with my grandfather. He stormed Omaha Beach when he was my age. He cried like a baby when we went back."

"Wow."

"*Saving Private Ryan*, you know the movie? He won't watch it. Do you like history?"

"I really do."

"Is it your best subject in school? It was mine."

"Well—" and here comes the embarrassing answer of the

year—"I'm homeschooled." Ugh! No matter how they all tell you how great it is, you can't help but feel mortified at offering up the information.

He says, "My mom homeschooled me for a year. It was all she could take! She took me to all the plays and museums, did seven subjects, and ran herself ragged. I had a great time, but I think she went a little overboard."

"Your mom sounds pretty cool."

"She is. I'm just glad she's around. She had cancer last year, but it looks like she's made it through."

"That's good."

"Definitely good."

He proceeds to ask me a thousand more questions and asks for more coffee even though I drank right from the thermos.

"So you seem older than high school," I say.

"Yeah, I am. I graduated from college last January. I did the fast track, overloaded my schedule, CLEPed a lot of classes, loaded up on summer school, and got out early. School was too confining."

"What are you doing on the film, then? Have you met Annette Bening yet?"

"No. She's not due in for another few days."

"I hear she's really nice."

For some reason, it's so important for me that people are nice.

"I've heard that too. Hey, I'd better go. I've got to be up before dawn."

"Well, don't come bother me then! I'm a night owl."

"Where are you staying?"

"Did you see that old Travco with the kitchen trailer?"

"No."

"I'm not surprised. It's on the edge of things. Anyway, if you see it, it's puke green and my mom painted a rainbow across the nose. It's really ugly, but I call it home."

He laughs. "I'll see if I can find it. If I can't . . . "

"I'll probably be back here again tomorrow night. Me and F. Scott." I point to the book lying on the sand.

He picks it up. "*The Great Gatsby.* I love this book. Have you seen the movie?"

"Which one?"

"Okay. You're a keeper. And there'll be yet one more Gatsby movie after all is said and done here." He hops to his feet. "Catch ya later. Maybe tomorrow night."

I screw the top back on the thermos.

"You don't have any real food in that Travco, do you?"

"What do you mean?"

"The food at the canteen is so . . . healthy. I just want a cheese-burger with American cheese."

"Or a grilled Velveeta sandwich?"

"I love Velveeta!"

"I don't think there's one natural thing in it."

"Me either. Hey, want to meet at Ten Clams in town tomor-row? I get off around four. I'll bet they have cheeseburgers. It looks very diner-like."

"Sure. Okay."

Soon he's gone.

Man, was he nice. See, that's the thing with film people: you never know what you're going to get.

Monday, April 5

I sneak back into the RV at two a.m. Despite the intrigue of Gatsby (and I'm really not sure how Annette Bening is going to fit into the story, as there are no grande dames in Fitzgerald's work, but then Hollywood doesn't care about accuracy) I fell asleep right there on the beach. Early April isn't exactly summertime in the Bahamas, people, and the icicles forming in my veins woke me up.

Why did that guy have to talk about cheese? It's all I can think about now.

Charley's still passed out, so I open the fridge and reach back into the corner and pull out a soy yogurt.

Bear with me.

I pry open the top and there it sits. Oh, joy! I bought it at the grocery store in town—a quarter-pound chunk of white cheddar. I always buy small increments in case Charley finds it. And always white, because I could pass it off as soy cheese or something. Charley wouldn't dream of getting the soy cheese with the red dye in it to orange it up. My teeth sink into the creamy goodness. I close my eyes, standing there in the light from the fridge.

How, oh how, do people like Charley go through life without this stuff?

"Do you know what time it is?" Charley's voice floats in from her sleeping compartment.

"Yeah, I was hungry."

"What are you eating?"

I hold up the container.

"Let me smell your breath."

Oh, crap.

"You're totally not serious, Charley."

"Oh yeah, I totally am."

"Come on. You're treating me like a little kid."

"Now!"

"Okay, okay." I *haaah* in her face.

"You were eating cheese again, weren't you?"

So busted.

Dear Elaine,

I just want to eat cheese. Is that so wrong?

Charley apologized this morning for getting on me about the cheese. I know it's one of her boundary lines, but I just don't see the point of not eating cheese. I mean, if God didn't want us to eat cheese, would he have let man invent it? Then again, he let man invent the atom bomb, and I'm sure he wasn't for that. But cheese is hardly a WMD, is it?

Don't even begin to argue with me on that one, Elaine. I know there are a lot of things we do that God, if he's at all worried about us down here, can't possibly think is all right. Ultra low-rise jeans, for one. Straightening irons, for two. Thong underwear, for a big three.

And the guy on the beach likes cheese too. Affirmation maybe? I think so. I felt a little embarrassed asking his name since he didn't ask mine. But he was nice. Hopefully he'll show up at Ten Clams as promised, although why he'd want to spend time with a frizzy-haired teenager in cat glasses is beyond me. Thank goodness there was no moon last night. He won't show.

I'll go anyway. Maybe Bob and Doris's niece will be around.

Okay, on to geometry. I hate geometry but I absolutely cannot blow off school again today. Charley's pretty good at math when she has the time. But that won't be anytime soon.

I don't blame her. She's made the best life she can. And I know she loves me.

Six hours later, after I wake up

Secondhand shops in small towns are the best places I know to find real vintage without paying overinflated prices. There's a cool little shop here on the island, so I park my scooter in front and wander around a wonderland of bright polyester. Truthfully, I like the natural fibers of the forties and fifties, but those are harder to find these days.

However, you never know. It's always worth a look.

I head over to the dress rack and start leafing through. Great prices, just like I thought. A full prism of color, and they sure weren't scared of a little color back in the day. Style? Oh they had style!

And there it hangs. Tucked between a White Stag parka and an olive-green and orange muumuu, a tulle prom dress in robin's-egg blue burgeons out. The bodice is embroidered with flowers and the back dips down into a shallow *V* with fabric-covered buttons lining up past the waist. Fifteen bucks.

Didn't I *just* say so?

Next the sweater rack—and behold! A little cardigan in pale green. A tiny hole opens up near the waistband, but that's okay. I can fix that. Eight bucks.

I could wear my biker boots with this, but that's hardly an unexpected choice these days. Ballet shoes. Most definitely.

The clerk is the owner, I suspect. He asks if I'm with the shoot and I say, "Sort of," and leave it at that.

"Do you know of a good place to get a grilled cheese sandwich?"

He folds up my purchases. "Ten Clams. Fabulous grilled cheese. And there's really not much else to choose from, obviously." He looks up into his hairline. "Let's see. The Windsor Hotel dining room and Blackbeard's Pub. Also the Veggie Garden."

"Vegetarian?"

"Vegan."

Good grief, they're taking over the world! "Ten Clams it is."

The clerk smiles and tells me to have a fabulous day as I exit the shop, bag hanging from the crook of my arm.

I walk my scooter down the small business district, the main street of the town called Galleon Street. A beachwear shop has yet to open for the season, as well as a caramel-corn and candy shop, and a sundries store selling all manner of suntan lotion, rafts, and bodyboards, if their window gives any clue.

Wouldn't it be fun to be here in the summer? But knowing Charley, we'll be somewhere in Alaska by then.

Oh, cool. According to the sign this little restaurant has Wi-Fi. Who knew a place called Ten Clams would be so up-to-date? Then again, the Grand Opening sign is a clue. So here we go. I get to meet Bob and Doris's niece, Joy Overstreet. And how in the world did she go from being a fashion designer to a waitress in an obscure diner at the edge of the world?

I brought my laptop with me to wrap up a history assignment I've given myself. I'm finishing a paper on the Vietnam war and how it might have been prevented. I've come up with some fascinating research about Ho Chi Minh. George Washington was his hero. Ho Chi Minh sought out Woodrow Wilson in Paris after World War I to mentor him and was rebuffed. Unfortunately, the communists in Paris deemed him worthy of their attention.

And so it goes.

I love history, but it's so sad. If only Wilson would have been nicer.

I finish the paper and plot my next assignment, this one on local lighthouses. They're all over the place out here.

Almost four o'clock. That guy won't show up. Maybe he's more the mysterious type like Gatsby, who threw these monster parties, where people got drunk, danced the Charleston in fountains on his estate, and ate rare foods, no doubt some of the best cheeses you could find. Gatsby would stay up in his rooms and watch from a distance.

Kinda creepy if you ask me. Personally, I think he was involved with the mob.

Then he'd venture outside to stare at the green light at the end of Daisy's dock. Are you kidding me? What was wrong with the man? Why do I love this book? I don't know. The only person worth a grain of salt is Nick the narrator. Go figure. But I do love it.

I check my watch every thirty seconds, which is stupid. I should just stare at it instead, like the green light on Daisy's dock.

It's a good watch. Five bucks. From the forties. I have to wind it, but sometimes there's a good thing about being responsible for your own time.

The new outfit might have been an okay choice, but it screamed "trying too hard," so I opted not to change out of the chocolate corduroys and a fisherman's sweater Charley's had around forever. But these clothes don't go with my glasses. At all.

The waitress, whose nametag says Angela, asks if I'm ready to order. "I'm waiting for someone."

"A drink?"

"Sure. Coffee?" That makes me look mature.

"Right-o."

"Hey, do you know Joy Overstreet?"

"I'm Joy."

"But your nametag—"

"I know! I'm—" she leans forward and whispers—"incognito these days."

"Gotcha." I lean forward and whisper. "Aunt Doris and Uncle Bob send their love."

"You know them?"

"Most definitely. See them on the road every once in a while in their RV."

I tell her a little about seeing them on I-40.

The bell on the door clangs against the glass and in walks, oh my gosh, Seth Haas!

I can't believe it! The blog's gonna be good tonight, baby!

Can I get him to talk to me? You think he might? I mean, it's not like he's a big star yet and has a million people approaching him or anything.

"Be right back with your coffee." Joy taps the table.

Okay, get a grip, Scotty. Just look at the menu.

I hold the menu up against my face as high as I can and peer over the top. He heads over to a table where a couple of girls are sitting and says something.

They shake their heads.

And then he notices me, sitting here in my booth, and . . . he's heading my way. Oh, crap. So I slide the menu up higher watching his feet move more closely from underneath the daily specials. Pumas, brown. Nothing special, a little worn. Cool though.

The Pumas stop and I look up over the top of my glasses, deciding to take the, "Hi. Can I help you?" approach.

He scratches the spot where his neck and shoulder meet just inside the blue collar of a tan T-shirt. "I don't know. I'm looking for someone."

"Somebody from the set?"

"How do you know I'm from the movie?"

"You're Seth Haas, aren't you?"

He shakes his head a little, jogging loose some marbles in there or something. "Yeah. How do you know that?"

"I saw you last summer in DC, *Much Ado about Nothing*. You were absolutely hilarious. Better than Michael Keaton was in the movie."

I don't tell him about seeing him in Connecticut. He might think I'm a stalker or something.

"Hey, thanks." He lowers his head, shakes it. "Oh, man. It's you, isn't it? I can't believe I didn't recognize your voice right off."

"I can't believe I didn't realize you were Seth Haas."

"I can't believe you've actually heard of me."

"I'm into the obscure. What can I say? You want to sit down?"

"Thanks. This is the first time I've been recognized by anybody." He takes a menu from between the sugar shaker and the napkin holder. "So I can't believe I forgot to ask your name last night."

"It's Scotty. Scotty Dawn."

"Pretty. Really nice to officially meet you."

"Me too."

"So do they have cheeseburgers?"

"Yeah. And grilled cheese. I already checked to see if they have American. They have white *and* yellow."

"Very nice." He sets down the menu.

I can't believe I'm acting so cool and confident. This is crazy!

Joy materializes, order pad in hand. "You all figure out what you want yet?"

How in the world did this woman go from being a fashion designer to a waitress in an obscure diner at the edge of the world? Seth gestures toward me.

"I'd like a cheeseburger, as rare as you'll make it, with a slice of white and a slice of yellow American cheese, lettuce, tomato, mayonnaise and mustard."

She turns toward Seth.

Seth! Seth Haas!

"And for you, sir?"

"Same, except no mustard and I'd like onions on that."

"Anything to drink?"

"Coffee," I say even though I already ordered.

"Same for me." Seth.

Then, "I'll have onions on mine too. Fried."

"Great." Joy turns around and heads over to the grill.

Okay, let me describe Joy before we get all into Seth Hott. She's heavy. Not way overweight, but definitely overweight. Her hair fountains out of a tight, high ponytail, very chichi, and her makeup is perfect. It's easy to see she was once a designer, even in the lime green shirt embroidered with the restaurant's logo, because her pants are just the right length to go with the cutest pair of black leather slides I've seen in a long time.

Back to the onions.

"I didn't want to blast you out," I said. "I love onions."

"Me too. And I don't care who knows."

"So yeah, I saw you in DC. And, don't get creeped out or anything, but I love literature and was really impressed with your portrayal of Dogberry, so I looked you up on the Internet. That's the only reason I'm familiar. And I'm a research junkie. I love finding stuff out."

"I'm not creeped out. It's pretty cool, actually. I've never had anybody recognize me before."

So he said.

"Get used to it."

"Yeah, like I'm going to make it really big."

"Oh, you are." I say it as if it's a curse.

"You think so?"

"I've been around this stuff long enough to know. For one, you're a nice looking guy; for two, you seem to work hard and not be all egocentric; for three, you actually can act. I mean look at how far a lot of guys have made it without numbers two or three."

He puffs air between his lips. "That sure is the truth."

"So yeah. But you'll be in the Johnny Depp realm — before he went so commercial."

"That would be fine with me. I'm under no delusion I'm the next Tom Cruise."

"Would you even want to be?"

"No. Not at all."

Joy brings us mugs of coffee, heavy, ivory ceramic mugs, so retro. "Here you go."

I take a sip. Okay, so here's the thing. I'm relatively isolated from society and I've learned to drink my coffee black because it's cooler. Who's even around to notice? Seth dumps two creams and a sugar into his.

I'm just sayin'.

"So, are you going to go into the Classical Acting Masters program at George Washington, then?" They sponsored the Shakespeare festival I attended.

"I'm enrolled and set to begin a year from September. I've got to save up some cash first."

"This movie should help, right?"

"Somewhat, sure. It's great money compared to slogging it out landscaping like I've done, but I'm a no-name. It won't set me up for life or anything."

Not everybody's getting rich in Hollywood. You can count on that, people!

I sip my coffee. "I sometimes get really mad at Charley, my mom, because we only work on these obscure, low-budget movies, but you know, she's remained a nice person. I can't help but think there's a connection between that and the fact that we've never become deeply embedded in Hollywood."

"No big surprise there." He leans forward. "I hate my agent. He's the biggest jerk in the world and he'll make me go as far as I can. But when I think about him speaking for me, I think, Oh, man, I hope my mom doesn't find out. Or my grandmother. That would really be awful. Especially Grandma, or should I say Grand Marion."

"Grand Marion?"

"Yes, that's actually what we call her."

"Assuming here her name's Marion."

"Yeah."

"Wow."

"I know. And it just says it all."

"A matriarchal family?"

He picks up his mug and raises it. "Oh yeah."

The hamburgers arrive and we pretty much eat everything on our plates without saying more than ten words apiece, including, "Pass the salt, please," and, "Should I ask for some ketchup?"

Finally, we push our plates aside, ask Joy for some more coffee, and decide to split a piece of coconut-custard pie.

"So what are those books you've got there? School stuff?" he asks.

"History mostly, plus some geometry. I've done all right on my own with most of this stuff, but math is my Achilles' heel."

"I'm not too bad at math."

"Really?" Should I ask him for help?

"I don't mean to presume or anything, Scotty, but you want me to help you with it?"

"That would be great."

"Okay, good. Then you can tutor me."

"What do you need tutoring for, Mr. I-Graduated-From-

College-At-Nineteen?"

He laughs, slipping a magazine out of his jacket pocket. *In Touch*. Only $1.99 at the grocery store, all any of those magazines are worth, but at least these people realize it. "I want you to tell me all you know about this stuff."

"I'm such an outsider, Seth."

"Exactly."

The restaurant is empty. Joy sits down next to me. "Can I see?"

"Sure," says Seth.

She sighs. "Look at those gowns."

I don't tell her I know her secret. I don't say, "What in the world are you doing waiting tables when you created some of the greatest fashions known to man?"

Poor Joy. Nobody leaves stuff like that behind without good reason.

Tuesday, April 6

Somebody's pounding on the trailer door. It's six a.m.

"Get up, kiddo!" a muffled voice yells from outside.

Jeremy? Jeremy!

"Woo-hoo!" I yell, jumping down from the bunk and flying to the door. In a display of affection that embarrasses the great director from his cowboy hat to the toes of his steel-tipped boots, I throw myself off the steps and into his arms.

"Good to see you, kiddo." He squeezes, then extricates

himself from my embrace, but in a nice way, saying, "Now listen to me. This is a tight shoot. I love you, Scotty. But I'm going to be busy. So don't take my lack of time as a lack of interest, okay?"

I hold my hand up to my mouth and howl with laughter. "You are the limit! Okay. I'll leave you alone. But promise me you'll make your stew for me when it all wraps."

"You got it. That's a plan."

Very cool.

"I feel terrible about this, kid, but I'll make it up to you when it's all over."

Later that evening, I hop down the steps of the Y.

The great film monster has taken over this sweet island. Barricades around the sets, trailers, our own security guard. The beach calls to me, telling me to escape. Seth joins me for a little while and checks over my geometry, helps me where I'd not completely understood, and watches while I figure it out, or try to, again, directing the beam of the flashlight onto the page. The air smells so salty.

I help him with *In Touch.*

"Okay, so Karissa Bonano hasn't arrived yet." He opens the magazine and points to her picture.

She smiles along with the latest celebrity heiress.

I don't know how to tell him this, but that Karissa is just a witch. She's been acting since before she was born, is twenty-one but as jaded as a fifty-year-old, I'll bet.

So before I'm seen as heartless, let me say I do feel sorry for these girls, but I also see firsthand how some of them treat people, and pity only goes so far toward the meanies of the world. I'm telling you, if everyone was just nice, the world would be a much better place to live in.

"Please don't tell me she's playing Daisy?"

"Yep." He jabs her photo with his index finger. "What should I expect?"

"Okay, first off, don't expect to do anything other than your job, all right? You're not going to impress her; she's been around Hollywood forever. You'll just be goofy if you try anything. Just show up, do your job, speak to her when spoken to, and then go home at the end of the day's shoot. That's it."

"That's it?"

"I'm telling you, Seth, you don't want to get yourself entangled in the webs of people like Karissa Bonano."

"Got it. Okay—" he flips to some another page—"explain this to me if you can."

"Jessica Simpson's edible makeup? You want an explanation for *that*?"

"Some things are unexplainable?"

"Welcome to Hollywood, Seth Haas."

Hollywood Nobody: April 6

Today's Rant: So raise your hand if you've seen bazillion-dollar actors talking about movie piracy. (Argh, mateys!) Yeah, you have? So why do they do that? Here: Instead of worrying about what everyone else is doing, A-listers, why don't you see what happens if you take half of what you're getting and put it in a fund for the lowly grips? Do you really think we're buying your ads? "Hello. I'm making twenty million dollars a picture and I'm worried about 'the little guy.'" Uh, okay. See who's the actor with the biggest mouth for the least buck after the jump.

Today's Quote: Proving again that there are some normal people in the film industry who see things for what they are. At least this time he did. "The nature of show business is people within the business feel that if someone else fails, they move up a notch." Tom Arnold

Today's Kudo: According to sources, The Nasty Baldwin Brother was left all by himself at Wolfgang Puck's when, after a particularly nasty rant at the waiter, his dinner partners walked out. Kudos to the dinner partners.

Today's News: Seth Haas has reported for duty. Here are pics of him as Dogberry in last summer's *Much Ado About Nothing* in DC. The scoop? He plans to get his masters in classical acting when he's amassed enough money to pay for it. Gotta love a guy this cute who's not content to rest on his chiseled jaw. But with that jaw, I'd say he'll have free pickin's on the money tree within two years tops.

Karissa Bonano should be on site soon. Stay tuned, Nobodies. This should be interesting.

Today's Disappointment: Mariah Carey lost all the weight. I truly thought she was beginning to celebrate the diva within. Wrong again! I can never quite tell what Miss Mimi is going to do.

Later, Nobodies!

Comments:

I love Mariah! She's got the best voice ever. — musicfiend, 3:45 p.m.

Mariah sucks! This blog sucks. — yeahbigtime, 5:00 p.m.

Thanks for this blog, nobody. I've sent my friends over here too. — hollywoodjunkie, 6:17 p.m.

I'm hollywoodjunkie's friend. She's right, Nobody. Love this! My mom has blocked all the other blogs because they're so skanky. — hollywoodjunkies_friend, 7:03 p.m.

Wednesday, April 7

Well, I got the guts to wear the vintage prom gown. It's chilly today, so I pulled on a pair of blue and green polka-dot tights and some black Chucks. So far so good. But I couldn't find a coordinating jacket. Consequently, I'm wearing Charley's wool Navajo poncho. Sometimes my obscurity is a downright blessing.

This outfit isn't hip, quirky, or funky. It's downright weird.

I throw my schoolbooks into a backpack and unlock my scooter from the nearby light pole. I'll cross the bridge over to Ocracoke and meet Joy Overstreet for real. She invited me to her place yesterday, wanting to hear all about Bob and Doris.

With my little digital camera, I'll take some pictures of the lighthouse too and start compiling my history unit. Lighthouses have always been one of my things. The whole idea comforts me, that there's a light keeper who knows where the shoals are and does his or her best to keep you from going under.

Okay, here's another embarrassing confession: I do all my history and social studies units in scrapbooks, complete with pretty stickers, die-cuts, fancy papers, gel-pen writing. It's very sad.

So add scrapbooking to my list of interests. Totally lame, but about as fun as you can get without the wind in your hair.

The breeze slices cleanly off the ocean and I try to go as fast as I can on the scooter, which isn't really anything more than a coughing fit compared to real vehicles clearing their throats and riding headlong into the wind.

So I cross the bridge from Toledo onto Ocracoke, Joy Overstreet's address in my backpack. Of course, I Google Mapped it yesterday. I head past the harbor, through town, and down one of the neighborhood streets. Overall, it's a little bigger than Toledo here, but just as sweet.

A mailbox resembling a beach cottage bears her house number. Oh, it's a cute place! Weathered and small, but almost as old as the island, or so it seems. It looks like one of those old life-saving stations the old-timers used to congregate at, waiting to rescue sailors from sinking ships. Big terra-cotta pots overflowing with pansies line up on the porch. Freshly mulched flowerbeds burgeon with yellow and purple crocuses, my favorite flower, a flower that lets the world know winter doesn't last forever.

I hurry up the steps, knock on the door.

A scream worthy of *Halloween* or even *Halloween II* resounds from inside the little home.

I knock again and yell, "Is everything okay?"

A few seconds later the door opens and there stands Joy, a cloud of ecru hair hovering above long earrings, five necklaces, and a black long-sleeved T-shirt that stretches across her bosom. Bare feet peek from beneath a circular skirt the color of pale-pink roses. "I'm about to drown my computer."

"Sorry."

"So come in and tell me how Aunt Doris and Uncle Bob look. I haven't seen them in at least a year."

She shows me into the house decorated in a homey yet chic fashion, walls washed in white, exposed rafters supporting cascading plants. I feel so peaceful in all the whites and creams. Charley loves neon colors.

"They're doing well. They were headed out to your cousin's graduation. In California."

"Sure. Brendan. Wish I could have gone. Things are tight."

"So what's happening with your computer?"

"I don't even know enough to tell you."

"Mind if I take a look?"

"It can't get any worse than it is already. Knock yourself out."

Joy leads me into the kitchen, where a small desk supporting a computer sits in the corner. "Have at it. Want something to drink?"

"Sure."

"Coke okay?"

"Real Coke?"

"Uh-huh."

Charley would have a fit!

"Yes, please. Thanks."

She yanks open a bright yellow sixties fridge, pops the top on a can of Coke and hands it to me. I take a long, amazing sip. "Have you lived here long?"

"A little while. It was my family's vacation home when I was a kid. My mom and dad bought it years ago . . . on their honeymoon!"

"Really?"

"Yes. We lived here every summer. I can't believe I'm going to have to sell it."

"Sell it? Why?"

"Waitresses don't make that much money. I borrowed against this place and can't pay it back."

"I'm really sorry."

"Yes, well, that's the way it goes sometimes, isn't it? Sometimes we never really do find a place we can call home for long. I should have never left New York."

"Tell me about it. You had some great creations."

"You heard of me? As a designer?"

"Most definitely."

"Well, that was two years and fifty pounds ago."

"I think you look great. Why did you leave the city?"

She looks over her shoulder. "I hated myself, Scotty. I was a really nice person when I went there. Then suddenly, I was a size two who could give her grandmother a dressing-down like you wouldn't believe. I had to get away."

"Most people don't have what it takes to do something like that. I mean walk away from the two Fs because it's killing them." Especially not on the brink of a grand success.

"True." She slides a kitchen chair out from under the table and sits down. "But some have what it takes to cope in the first place."

"And you didn't."

"Not even a little bit."

I look up at her over the tops of my glasses. "So what you're telling me is that it doesn't get easier?"

"Not remotely."

"Great."

Turning back to the keyboard, I power down the computer. At least Joy's honest and open. After living with Charley, I'm going to enjoy that.

I stay for lunch, help her clear off all of the files she doesn't need anymore, and we laugh and talk about our favorite old designers. Joy is delighted and calls me a kindred spirit.

I'm just sayin'!

A few hours later

I set down the book as Seth walks up to the blanket.

"Hey, Scotty."

"Hey."

"You got any coffee tonight?"

"Sure." I reach into my backpack for an extra cup and pour some coffee into it. "How's it going over there? Charley didn't have to take anything with her. She said they were shooting on Ocracoke at the lighthouse."

A night shoot. Which is why I'm here on the beach when I shouldn't be.

"Yeah, we were. We're doing the scene where Daisy and Jay see each other for the first time in a while." He groans and sits down.

"No kissing in that scene then."

"Nah. Not yet."

"I'm surprised they didn't change that too."

"Me too."

I hand him his coffee.

"You know, Scotty, I had no idea there was this much waiting around. I mean yeah, you sort of figure it's not all shoot, edit, and out the door it goes, but good grief."

"Hence the trailer. Do you have your own trailer? Jeremy's pretty low-budget."

"No. No trailer. I didn't expect one, to be honest."

"I don't know if Bening will even have one. Everybody works with Jeremy for the artistic prestige. I'm kinda surprised he's using Karissa Bonano. I've never thought of her as a particularly talented actress."

"Let's just say the part isn't a real stretch for her: spoiled, vapid child of a rich family."

"Got it."

"Yeah. So let's not talk about the film."

"But are you enjoying it?"

His smile shines in the darkness. "Oh yeah. It's almost like a drug."

I sip my drink. "And you know, you're really smart to start out in one of Jeremy's films if you want to be seen as one of those young actors with artistic integrity, not just 190 pounds of beefsteak."

The coffee practically spews out of his mouth. "Scotty, you're hilarious. No chance of getting a big head with you around."

"Uh, *no*. Not even a little bit. For one, I'm overexposed. For two, I've never known anything else. For three, stick around long enough and you'll know exactly what I mean."

"So. How'd geometry go today?"

"I think I did a little better. Would you mind checking my work tomorrow?"

"Not at all."

We sit in silence, listening to the waves breaking along the shoreline (a more peaceful sound I've yet to hear) and I think about tomorrow morning, April 8, how the sun will rise over this ocean and trigger Charley's tears. She always cries on April 8.

"What?" I say. "Sorry, I didn't hear you."

"Yeah, you were spaced. What're you thinking about? You had this really sad look on your face."

I sigh and lay back on the blanket. "Tomorrow's April 8th. My mom cries off and on all day. She does this one day in September too. I have no idea why." I sit up and look at him. "Do your parents have any secrets, like big secrets, that you know about?"

"Nah. We're pretty average America, Scotty. I have no idea what that must be like. My mom's a real-estate agent and Dad's the music teacher at the local middle school. Stephen and Edie are about as open-book as you get."

"Are they nice?"

"Totally."

"It must be fun to come from a regular background with regular parents."

He shrugs. "I've never really thought about it like that, Scotty. I mean, a lot of people would think your life sounds pretty cool. No strings, riding with the wind and stuff."

I laugh. "It sucks."

"Yeah, maybe."

"Trust me."

He leans back on his elbows. "I don't know. It's got to have its good points, if you let it. I mean, it is what it is, right?"

He's telling me to suck it up and look on the bright side. But how could Mr. Middle America begin to know what it's like? "Yeah. It is what it is."

"I'm sorry your mom's so sad."

"What I'm scared about is what it'll be like for her when I go off to college. I'm all she has and even I'm not completely enough, right? When I'm gone, what will happen to her?"

"I don't know. But people have a way of adapting."

I think about our RV, our nomadic life. "With Charley, who knows what that'll look like?"

Seth leans forward and hugs me. His arms warm me. He squeezes and sits back. "It'll be all right. People do crazy things, but in the end it somehow all works out."

He must be a religious nut. They always say that sort of stuff. "Do you believe in God, Seth?"

"Yeah. My folks are really into church. I used to be but kinda got away from it all in college."

"I've only been to church a couple of times. There's going to be a tent meeting here soon. I'm going to check it out. I'm making it part of my school history unit. You know tent meetings used to be really big deals."

"I've been to a couple myself."

"Really?"

"Sure. All this shouting and jumping around and healing and all."

"Healing? They do healing at those things?"

"The ones we went to. My parents are really into all that Pentecostal stuff. I think that might have been my problem. I never felt comfortable. But I did learn a lot about theatrics!"

"Seth! That's horrible."

"Tell me about it. My parents are going to be visiting soon. Don't you dare tell them I said that!"

"Maybe they'll be here for the tent meeting."

"That would be crazy, wouldn't it?"

"I am going, you know."

He holds up his hands, palms forward. "Hey, I'm not going to stop you."

Thursday, April 8

So I'm back at Ten Clams. With the free Wi-Fi and not-so-bad coffee available, I have made this spot my hangout.

Joy walks over with the coffeepot. "I enjoyed your visit."

"Me too. I've been thinking a lot about what you said. About turning into someone else when you were in New York. So are you going to be a waitress forever or are you gearing up to do something else?"

Joy sits opposite me in the booth. "Oh, I'm trying on all sorts of things for size. In my mind."

"Like what?"

"I'm thinking about going to court-reporter school."

"You're kidding! With your talent?"

She rolls her eyes. "Or I could be a barber. Or even a nail technician."

"Order up!" the cooks yells.

"They're playing my tune," she says and hurries back to the kitchen.

I open up my browser, Google "tent meetings" and learn that "Revival is in the land!" I have no idea what that means, but there are these guys that go around and set up their tent and talk about the river Jordan and Joshua and all. According to their website, people are being healed and what can a person make of all that? Maybe the people at this church here will be doing the same sort of thing and I can see for myself.

So here's the deal: a lot of people need all this proof that something's real. I've taken the Internet's word on things for years, so I can't claim to be one of those kind. Experience goes farther with me when it comes to proving anything. Facts are a little dry when you lay your head down at night in an RV and wonder who your dad is and why your mother is sad and a little distant, why there are people out there who think because they're famous they can treat you like dog doo. I mean, you don't get a pass on manners because you're rich, do you?

I've decided my new hero is John Wesley, quite possibly the father of tent meetings. The Wesleyans have done a lot of tent meetings, which stemmed from Wesley's habit of preaching in the open air, in other ministers' churches, and even in a graveyard. He used his father's tombstone as a pulpit.

I wonder if my dad has a tombstone.

The way I see it, Wesley and I know a little bit about discouragement—he didn't exactly have it easy. But the guy had faith. I really do think you've got to have faith if you want any hope of making it in this world. But faith in what? I guess that's the biggie.

I've watched a lot of preachers on television and they seem to have it all together: nice suits, expensive ties, pretty sons and daughters. But Wesley had obstacles to climb over and didn't let them stop him.

Seth's right. I could stop being so whiney and maybe start being a little more thankful. Maybe my life really is cool. I mean, how many teenagers enjoy this kind of freedom, this Bohemian groove factor?

And every once in a while, people like Seth, and Grammie and Grampie and Bob and Doris come along to make me feel like I'm not so completely alone.

Especially Grammie and Grampie.

"I thought I'd find you here."

I look up. "Oh, hey Seth. You want to sit down?"

"Yeah. I've got two free hours. So, is this your new hangout?"

"Most definitely." He is just so cute. I mean, really. Today he's wearing an orange T that says, "AWESOME at Ping-Pong!" with a ball whizzing across the plain of his chest.

"Excuse me!" he calls over to Joy. "You got a fresh pot of coffee?"

"Sure thing, babe."

I lean forward. "She thinks you're cute."

"You think so? Really?"

"Oh yeah. Are you blind?"

"She's kinda cute herself."

"She's at least thirty, Seth."

"I know, but you know what they say about older women."

"No. Fill me in." It's fun making him squirm.

"Well, I don't know really. I thought you did." He laughs.

"Nicely done. You just remembered I'm only almost sixteen."

"Yeah. You seem a lot older."

"Thanks. I think."

"Oh, no! That was definitely a compliment."

Joy sets down a mug of coffee.

"Thanks, Angela," Seth says. She makes a beeline for the kitchen.

Oh, brother.

"Her name's Joy, by the way."

"But doesn't her name—"

"Yep."

He shakes his head.

"So can I show you my geometry?"

"Bring it on, sister."

Sister? He called me sister. No one's ever called me sister before.

I like it.

"Hey," I say, "the little grocery store has Velveeta. Charley's got a really busy day tomorrow and I'm going to make myself a grilled Velveeta for dinner."

"You're planning this in advance?"

"We all do what we must."

"Can I have one?"

"Are you kidding me? What time?"

"I'll be free after three thirty."

"Okay." I pull out my math papers and he begins to rip apart my work.

"You got a red pen, Scotty?"

"A red pen?! What are you, some kind of college professor or something?"

"Okay, a pencil then."

"Here." I roll one across the table and he begins to go to town. Great, just great.

"You've got some more work to do."

"Darn. I thought I was just beginning to understand."

"Oh, you are. It's a lot better than what you were doing before, but it's still off."

And so he begins to explain, and explain and explain, and after five minutes all I can think about is that typing exercise, "Now is the time for all good men to come to the aid of their country." It resounds in my head over and over.

His mouth moves but I hear nothing.

"Okay, stop, Seth. I've begun to zone."

"We'll review more of it tomorrow over Velveeta."

"I think that's a good idea."

Joy sneaks up with her order pad. "You all want something other than coffee? The peach pie's great. I made it myself." She looks down at my paperwork. "Oh, I'm a wiz at math!"

"Well, Seth isn't having much luck tackling me on his own. Maybe between the two of you something will jog loose in this thick head of mine."

"Sounds good to me. Hey, why don't you come over for supper this evening? I could help you, and I could sure use the company."

We arrange a time.

She fiddles with one of her pretty necklaces.

"Are those semiprecious stones?" I ask. I got into stringing beads one time, bought a bunch made out of semiprecious stones like amethyst, amber, and garnet, and called it a science unit.

"Yep. I just love them."

"You made those?" They're more than strung beads I'll tell you. Wire curled into flowing shapes, wrapped around and around, beads hanging down, all arranged in a pleasing, balanced willy-nilly.

"Yep."

"Are they for sale?"

"I'm in such a spot right now I'll sell just about anything."

Sounds like a lot of people in the film industry.

Hollywood Nobody: April 8

Today's Rant: Producers who encourage actresses to look like smiley faces on a stick. I'd like to know what these guys look like themselves. I swear it's misogyny at its finest. So much for women's liberation, girls. Ladies, you're setting us back years with all these diets and surgeries, these "anorexic adult-film-star" ideals, and yes, you're responsible. Don't talk to me about not wanting to be a role model. You are one. Get over it. Tell those fat bald guys in the offices to take a hike, you'll eat what you like. Tell your stylists, "No thanks, I'd rather look like a normal human being."

Today's Kudo: <u>Annette Bening</u> arrived today looking like a goddess. If she's had surgery, it's wonderful and appropriate. She looks fresh but still in her forties. And pleasant. A friend of mine from a past shoot always says, "At my age, all I can hope for is pleasant." In Bening, pleasant meets beautiful. She'll be her generation's Jessica Tandy, and I can't think of a better person to be compared to. More on Tandy <u>here</u> if you don't know who she was.

Today's Seth Haas Tidbit: He's smart, Nobodies! He graduated with honors and a double major in drama and journalism at the age of nineteen. Graduated high school at sixteen. The boy asks a LOT of questions and Little Me ain't telling how I know. For now, he's a nice guy with high hopes. What will Hollywood do to him? Stay tuned to find out what he's made of.

Later!

Comments:

Well, I'm a naturally skinny person and I try to put on weight but still stay slender. I can't help it if I'm a size zero. Are you saying we look bad? — babygirl, 10:14 p.m.

No. We just wish you'd be quiet about your skinniness. We don't feel sorry for you. We don't want to hear it. Just be thankful and be quiet. — hollywoodjunkie, 1:03 a.m.

Amen, Junkie! Just shut up, Baby. — Me_too, 6:40 a.m.

Now, now, folks! — hnobody, 8:26 a.m.

Later

Is there no shame left in the world? I mean, come on! After Seth left the restaurant I stayed behind, blogged, wrote more on

Wesley, found out about Toledo Island and Ocracoke, and I'm definitely going to visit the ghost town on the desert island of Portsmouth soon.

A ghost town. Now that sounds like something out of the norm.

So I was walking back toward the RV when I passed these girls sitting near the canteen, drinking smoothies or some dreck like that and holding pocket mirrors up to their noses.

The twins.

They're playing the young cousins of Seth's Gatsby character in the movie. Jeremy created secondary parts like these to make it feel more contemporary. I told Charley, "Yeah, a contemporary Disney Channel Movie." These girls used to be on Nickelodeon, still are probably, and they must be pretty good actresses if Jeremy's using them, but still, they sat at a picnic table comparing nose jobs.

I kid you not.

They're about thirteen years old.

Now what surgeon would give a thirteen-year-old a nose job?

I tell Charley about it as we eat our supper. She reached an all new low. Whole-wheat pasta should be outlawed as far as I'm concerned. It tastes so grainy, yet carries a hint of slime, and pasta should be smooth like they do it in Italy, right? I mean, how many Italians eat whole-wheat pasta? And it's their thing, right? Shouldn't they know? I'm definitely *not* going to research that one!

"What do you think of all that?" I don't know why I'm asking her. You can tell Charley was absolutely gorgeous in her day. She still turns heads and, though she's in her midfifties, she's only just started thinking about her biological clock.

"I think it's silly to have plastic surgery that young. Kids grow into their noses. You know? But who am I to judge? We can't know how they feel about themselves, the pressures they face, Scotty. Can you imagine being in their shoes?"

"No."

"I know you don't have the most normal of childhoods, but to be expected to perform? Imagine trying to please other people all the time like that. It's got to be terrible for them."

"But those girls can be so mean!" I've been twirling the same bit of pasta around my fork for minutes now hoping she won't notice.

"It's a defense mechanism, I'm sure."

"Why do their moms let them do this stuff in the first place?"

"They've got their own issues, I guess."

Still. "Yeah, but wouldn't you think they'd want to do what's best for their child in the long run?"

Charley looks up and I see all the years that normally don't ride on her face jump aboard. "Yes, Scotty, you'd think that."

And that's as close to judgmental as Charley will ever get. But I needed it. I needed to know she's at least trying to do what's best. Given the circumstances. Whatever they are.

"I need to ask you a question, Charley, and I need an answer."

"I don't know if I can promise you that."

"I need to know if your sadness and your secrecy are because of me."

"Yes. And no. It's more than a little complicated."

"Are you trying to do what's best for me?"

"Yes. Yes. Yes. And that's God's honest truth, baby. Eat that bite please. You're driving me nuts with all that twirling."

"Okay. Okay." I fork the pasta into my mouth. It's still slick cardboard with sauce, but she's trying, isn't she? She's doing the best she can with what life has handed her.

That's all each of us can do.

Dear Elaine,

I talk all big on the blog, but if you want to know the truth, I'm jealous of those girls. They're beautiful, and at the end of the day, does it really matter how they got that way? I look at my frizzy hair, my weak eyes, and yes, the glasses are cool, but it puts me into that "artsy yet not at all alluring" category. Hardly California. Say what you will, Elaine, but a tan, skinny body and long blond hair always win in the looks department. At least at my age. At least that's what I think.

Then again, Catherine Zeta-Jones beats all.

I will admit that a woman trying to look all Malibu Barbie into her forties and beyond tips the scale over to the pathetic.

But I'm not forty. I'm only almost sixteen and I know a guy like Seth is out of my league, but I'd like a little bit of *intriguing* and *pretty* to carry around with me, even if I'm too young for him to ever consider. I'd like him to think, "It's a shame she's only fifteen," which I'm sure he doesn't. I'll bet that thought has never even crossed his mind.

Friday, April 9

Charley crosses her arms and eases down into a lime green camp chair next to mine. I've made us a nice, homey campsite, complete with a fire pit and an azalea bush from the garden shop. "Please, Scotty, I wouldn't ask you if it wasn't an emergency, you know that."

Drat. It had been so nice with the sun shining down, everything so quiet, and I was researching Wesley, who actually brewed his own beer. I wouldn't be surprised if he made his own cheese, and if he did, well, he's *surely* my new hero.

"I know, but Charley, it's never something fun. They never make me up to look beautiful. What's the part I have to play?"

"A waving mustard."

"A waving mustard? What's a waving mustard?"

She leans down like I'm a toddler or something, getting on my level. "You wear a costume that just slips over your head, a character costume that looks like a squeeze bottle of mustard. You won't even see your face."

"Of course not. You can never see my face when I do this. Charley! Are you sure there's no one else?"

"Not right now. And I mean *right now*. They want to shoot the scene in thirty minutes. It would save Jeremy a bundle if you would."

"Will he pass some of the savings down to me?"

She crosses her arms. I shut the laptop with a sigh. "All right. Let me put my computer away. Do I need to report to Ms. Burrell?"

"Yep. Thanks, baby. You're fab!"

Fab. Yeah. That would be me.

Five minutes later I knock on the wardrobe trailer.

"Come in if you're Scotty! If you're not Scotty then leave me be, I tell you!"

"It's me, Ms. Burrell."

I love Ms. Burrell. We've worked on at least ten films together.

Ms. Burrell is brown, the hue of German chocolate cake, and honestly, she's bleached her hair to a shade of toasted coconut, and it sticks out of her head like shaved coconut too. She's just as sweet as cake, but only if you're not in her way. If you get in her way when she's busy . . . well, just don't. My advice? Walk into heavy traffic against the stoplight instead. You're less likely to get hurt.

I step up into a miniature wonderland of fabric and trim, clothing crammed on rods going down the entire length of the trailer. Her machines are bolted to a table at the opposite end. She runs her life like Charley runs hers. On the road, indie film to indie film. Little theater productions too. A real independent-minded woman! "I work cheap because I keep my expenses small. And that takes sacrifice!" she always says. Her dog is a Chinese crested hairless. The ugliest doggone thing you've ever seen. Thankfully, Lolita sleeps all the time.

"Please tell me Charley got it wrong."

"Oh, child, I wish I could." She stands up, all who-knows-how-many pounds of her, and I have to admire her for loving her food despite the fact that she works with human kindling all day long.

She tromps up to the door, reaches behind a rack of clothing, and pulls out a fluorescent-yellow soft-sided creation, a barrel of mustard with a red-coned cap for easy dispensing. Her arms jiggle and flow.

"Do I need to change?"

"Naw, jeans are fine. Now lift your arms, there we go." She swings it over my head. "And put your hands through those armholes. Good. Can you see out that little mesh window?"

"Unfortunately, yes. This is humiliating."

"I know. But it's for a good cause."

"I'd like to know what that is."

"Art."

I snort. "Have you ever read *To Kill a Mockingbird*, Ms. Burrell?"

"Mercy, yes! Are you thinking of yourself as Scout in that ham costume?"

"Yeah. Big time."

And she begins to laugh, and laugh and laugh. When Ms. Burrell starts laughing the whole world should really stand still and take notice. It's that much fun.

She swats where my behind would be. "Get on over there. They're on Galleon Street near the veterinary hospital. You know it? It's only a couple of blocks away. Next to the video arcade."

"Yeah."

"Oh, and don't forget the gloves."

She slides balloonlike Mickey Mouse gloves on my hands. And so the trek of agony begins.

Not many people take notice really. I mean, work around film for long, and a walking mustard isn't all that strange. But still. I pass the canteen and there sits Seth with Karissa Bonano and she's pushing her chest all out at him and smoothing her long blond California hair.

Thank goodness for this suit. I never pictured a scenario where I'd be thankful to be wearing a mustard suit, but this really is it!

"Hey, Scotty! See ya later for those sandwiches!" Seth calls.

I wave one of my cartoon hands and keep walking. I can't think of one single thing in the world that would make me stop. Not a missile attack, a tidal wave, a tractor-trailer bearing down on me. Not wealth, not beauty, not fame, not a photographic memory.

Okay, maybe I'd stop for a photographic memory.

So a few minutes later I stand on the corner of the scene and wave and wave. Hello, film world, I'm a mustard. Just a big old squeeze bottle of mustard, standing on the corner, always destined to be hidden inside, anonymous, and just plain weird.

And how in the world did Seth know it was me in this suit?

Sandwich time

"The mustard just walked like you, Scotty. I don't know. I just knew it was you. Don't ask me why."

"Was it my shoes?"

"I've never noticed your shoes before. I don't know."

Drat. He's never noticed my shoes. See? I'm on his Little Sis radar, and that's about it.

"Okay. Anyway, I'm glad you didn't make an issue of it and make me stop. That would have been humiliating with Karissa Bonano sitting right there."

"Why?"

"I don't know. She's gorgeous for one thing."

"Karissa? You're kidding me, right?"

I reach into the RV fridge for the Velveeta. I asked Ms. Burrell to keep Charley occupied for a couple of hours, so she invited my mom to the cottage she's sharing with some other crew members. I hand him the cheese.

"Oh, please!" He slaps the orange box on the counter. "All that time she must spend in the tanning booth? She's going to look like Grand Marion's old pocketbook in twenty years. And her looks are kind of obvious, Scotty. Barbie-like. I really prefer a deeper, more ethnic kind of beauty."

"Like Penélope Cruz?"

"Yeah. But even in European girls, it's neat to see features still close to their origins. Like you. You're so Irish it isn't even funny. You've got that broad face, those deep eyes and a small mouth. Your skin is so fair and pink."

Oh my gosh.

"See what I mean? Karissa looks like a million other girls over here who are bowing to mass hysteria."

"Mass hysteria?" I laugh and he joins in.

"The sad thing is, they're so much prettier in their natural state."

Seth lays a hand on my arm. It's a beautiful hand, nails clipped short but not manicured, fine dark hairs lightly covering the back, what I imagine an artist's hands would look like. I feel a river of warmth flow from his touch to someplace deep inside. "Scotty, don't fall for this stuff. Please. You're smart and really, really pretty. I know you're still young, but hang onto who you really are, babe."

He called me babe.

I look up into his face and see a tender smile. The smile, truly, of a brother. I always wanted a brother. Especially a nice one like Seth.

"Okay. It's hard, you know? I don't know about this stuff. My life . . . it's so . . ."

"Strange?" He opens up the cheese.

"Closed up. Film people and RVers, Seth. How am I supposed to figure life out from these groups?"

"I'd say you're already ahead of the game. You're doing fine, Scotty. You really are."

I smile sideways. "If you say so." We've got to get off this subject. "Hey, I smuggled in some bacon, but I have no idea how we're going to cook it and not have Charley smell it as soon as she walks in the door."

"You got a grill?"

"Sure. A little hibachi underneath."

"Then leave the bacon to me."

I should tell him the bacon's going to slip right through the grid, but I won't be the one to squash his enthusiasm. "Go right ahead. I'll make us up a couple of limeades."

"Limeades? I love lime."

Of course he does. I found this out on the Internet, but I'm not going to let him know I know that.

"Me too."

So he fires up the grill while I crack ice with the back of a spoon like Grammie does when she makes lemonade, pour in Sprite, and squeeze in several limes. I've got to say, it's some of the best stuff that will ever slide down a throat.

I don't know how he managed it, but Seth comes back in with a plate of perfectly cooked bacon.

"It didn't slide through the grill?"

"Hey, I'm a master at this stuff. I've been grilling with my dad forever."

He hands me the plate and I begin to assemble the sandwiches. The skillet heats up on the stove.

"So have you ever had a girlfriend? Drink's on the table in the red cup."

He picks up the limeade. "Not anybody truly serious. I've gone out on dates and stuff, but I guess I'm a hopeless romantic." He sips the drink. "Wow, this is great!"

"Thanks."

"So . . . romantic how, Seth?"

"My parents have a great marriage."

"Lucky them."

"Not at all! They got divorced when I was five and found their way back together through a lot of hard work on both their parts. I'd like a woman as strong as my mom, to forgive my dad like she did."

"She'll be almost impossible to find. Especially at your age."

He breaks a piece of bacon in half and hands me one of the pieces. "You're so right. I guess I'm content to wait awhile. Most girls aren't worth the struggle a relationship entails."

"That's pretty cynical. Maybe there's somebody. Some pretty girl you just won't be able to resist."

"No thanks."

He's too good to be true. What's going to happen to him when temptation truly strikes? He's so level-headed now. But I've seen them come and go along this road, and it's amazing how easy it is to fall in line, let go, and become just another Hollywood hottie.

Don't let that happen to him.

I breathe in. Who was I talking to just then? I'll think about that later.

"So you said you dated a lot?"

"Not a lot. But I did. Made a couple of mistakes along the way."

Translation: had sex and regrets it.

He sets down the drink. "Don't make some of the mistakes I did, Scotty. It's totally not worth it."

"Like I even have opportunity."

"You will. But you're better than all that, Scotty. A girl like you can go so far. You don't have to throw yourself in front of some train wreck of a guy who doesn't respect you."

"Did you not respect those girls?"

"No. I didn't."

At least he's honest.

Hello Elaine,

Do I get the mustard parts because I'm not pretty? Is Seth telling me all this stuff just to let me down easy into the fact that I'm better off without sex because sure as rain falls from the sky there isn't one guy out there who would touch me with a ten-foot pole?

Hey, but at least we exchanged cell-phone numbers tonight. I mean, that's something, right?

Saturday, April 10

The engine thrums to life and I raise my head. "Charley?"

"Road trip, Scotty! Go back to sleep!"

"Where are we going?"

"Cape Charles, Virginia. On the Eastern Shore!"

At least she knows where it is. "You do know where it is, don't you?"

"I've got directions from Jeremy. He needs me to scout out the place for a possible location. We'll be there in about five hours."

I decide to go ahead and fall back asleep. Another night commute with Charley. She's been doing this ever since I can remember. We're not scouting out a location. Oh, she'll pretend to and we'll walk around the streets, look in antique shops, have a nice meal to placate me for all the food I eat squirreled away in an RV, and she'll let me choose whatever I'd like.

But I know better.

Tell me something, Charley! Tell me what it is that makes you sad, keeps us running, and drives us into the darkness at a moment's notice.

Seth and I stayed up until three, sitting with the crabs on the beach. I would tell Elaine that I'm feeling my heart break under the strain of an impossible love, but some things you can't even write in your diary.

Good night.

The hum of the road isn't all that bad, actually.

Six hours later

I've got a good handle on my geometry homework by the time we pull into Cape Charles and, naturally, I've already researched the town a little bit: built for the railroad and ferry industries in the late eighteen hundreds, a well-preserved Victorian town. Very nice.

Charley turns the RV onto Fulcher Street and stops. "Okay, this is your weekend. There are two places Jeremy told me about, The Nottingham Inn, which is on the Bay: secluded, burning sunsets over the water, wildfowl and all that. Or, we can stay in town at the Kellogg House: really luxurious, and a suite is open."

"How do you know all this already?"

"Jeremy called ahead for me."

"Charley, you're going to have to fess up one of these days about Jeremy. You're totally in love with him."

She blushes. "Which one?"

"In town! Definitely!"

"I knew you'd say that!" She pulls forward and takes a left onto Monroe Avenue. "This'll be fun, baby. We really need time to get back in the groove with each other. You know?"

"Yeah."

"I mean, I know I've been really busy and we've gone from movie to movie, and I've been working out a deal on the phone."

"Is that what you've been doing?"

"Uh-huh. Sure."

She's so lying. It's more important than just a deal.

But she's excited and I don't want to ruin the weekend. We're staying at an inn. Real shower, high thread-count sheets, and mints on your pillow. "So there'll be a bathtub, right?"

"Yeah, man!"

She holds out her hand and I give her "some skin."

I love my mother so much, but she hides herself from me. How do you deal with something like that?

Once we're settled in our suite—yes, *suite*—painted in shades of white and cool green, peppered with antiques and lots of windows, she walks onto the sun porch and dials her phone. "Why don't you figure out where we can go for lunch?" she calls.

Are you kidding me? This I can do.

She's talking to Jeremy, I can tell. Yeah, she does love the guy, but why he's this famous director and she's just the food stylist, following him around from film to film, I don't know. It's not that he doesn't respect her or anything. Jeremy loves my mother in his odd, artsy way, and he's obviously looking out for her.

Soon we're sitting in the Harbor Grill looking out over the Chesapeake Bay. It's funny, but Jeremy seems to be drawn to the water. A lot of his films are set near a body of water, mostly the ocean or large rivers and lakes. He seems bent on detailing simple life in profound locations.

And then there are his edgy pieces done in cities. The latest is an ongoing project, every year shooting a little more, and what he will unveil and when is anybody's guess. Even Charley doesn't know what that's all about.

In this moment, Charley looks even younger than usual. "Whew! What a relief to be away from that set. I don't know why Jeremy had to do a film with so much partying. So much food! It is funny though. That Seth friend of yours has a real way with humor."

"Really? Is he really good?"

"Yes. Funny but subtle. Like a really, really amazing Ashton

Kutcher. Kind of like Ashton Kutcher and Robert Downy Jr. crash together and end up as Seth."

Uh, okay then, Charley.

"Did you say *funny*?" I ask.

"Yep."

"Isn't it *The Great Gatsby*?"

She blinks at me. Okay, then.

"He's a really nice guy." I open my menu and lean forward. "Can I order anything I want?"

She smiles. "Yeah, Scotty. Eat all the cheese you want."

I order mozzarella sticks for starters, then beer-cheese soup. And for my meal, the three-cheese quiche with crabmeat. And yep, they've got cheesecake for dessert.

Nice.

Charley wants to hear all about my life. So I fill her in on Joy Overstreet, despite the obvious discomfort Charley exhibits at my leaving the campsite without permission. I explain that Joy needs more work.

Her eyes widen and she points her fork at me. It's loaded with spinach salad. "You know that Ms. Burrell's drowning in the wardrobe trailer and—" she leans forward—"Karissa Bonano said she was a size zero and she's a two. She's having to let out almost everything. Want me to talk to Jeremy about it?"

"You think he'd give her work? Come on, Charley, Jeremy's tighter than Joan Rivers's eyelids."

She laughs. "Let me ask."

My phone beeps.

"What's that, Scotty?"

"Text message."

"Really?"

I can tell she's trying not to freak, because I'm so not allowed to give anybody my phone number, and I am so busted!

"It's from Seth, I'll bet. I swear, Charley, I haven't given it out to anybody else."

She looks down and breathes in through her nose. "Go ahead and check it."

Where r u? u all right?

I punch in a reply.

Fine. With mom for weekend away.

I look up. "Will we be back tomorrow night?"

"We should be."

Be back tomorrow night. See you Monday?

I hit send. "So I'm sorry. He asked and I just blurted it out."

"It's okay. You've got to have some sort of life, you know. I just . . ." She folds her napkin in half and in half again. "It's okay, Scotty. It's okay."

The phone beeps.

C u mnday night w the ghost crabs?

I'll be there.

With coffee?

I punch in the final message.

With coffee.

Hey, might as well plant a seed while the field's fertile. "Does this mean I can eat cheese for good now?"

"Don't be going all crazy on me at once!"

I take that as a no.

But soon we're talking about what's going on in the film, laughing until we cry, and I remember why I'm glad she's my mother. You read the tabloids and see how crappy parents can be. Charley's never brought a guy home, slept with him, and expected me to understand she's "in love."

Even if I played sports, she wouldn't sit on the sideline with somebody who wasn't my dad and make out like Mission Impossible Man and The President's Daughter.

I'm just sayin'.

Then again, she's totally flipped out over Jeremy, so who knows what they do when nobody's looking?

An older couple sips drinks at the table across from ours. She looks up and smiles, lips overlaid with azalea pink. "You all having a nice mother-daughter lunch?"

"Yes," I say.

"You sure look like you have a good time together."

We are now, I think.

Charley says, "I'm very fortunate."

After paying the bill we take a walk.

We're sitting by the bay on a wide stretch of sand.

"Did you and your family ever go on vacation, Charley?"

"Yep. Every summer Mom packed up the car and we'd drive down to the bay—"

"This bay? The Chesapeake?"

"Of course. My aunt had a big old cottage on the island of Wenona. We'd swim all day, have corn roasts at night, steam crabs, and my sisters and I would sleep outside on the porch."

Sounds like heaven on earth.

"And then we'd get up the next morning, eat a bowl of Cheerios, and do it all over again. For a month."

"Where was your father?"

"He was at work. He worked for the gas company, but he'd come down on the weekends."

"How come you don't talk about your past? Why don't I know

as much as a daughter should about her mother?"

A sailboat slips by in the distance, graceful and free. So opposite from who I am.

"We'd sail on the bay then, and I remember thinking how I'd like to be free." She turns to me. "I grew up in a little two-bedroom house in Brooklyn. It's a real blue-collar neighborhood in Baltimore. My mother married beneath her, as they used to say in those days."

"She was from a rich family?"

"Yeah. Hence my aunt's summer home. It was the same old story you hear, Scotty. My grandfather threatened to disinherit her if she married my dad. She did anyway. And he called her bluff. So there we were, tucked away in that neighborhood, crawling all over each other. Mom and Dad in one bedroom, my sisters and I in another. We'd catch the bus to St. Rose of Lima School downtown and come back home to crawl all over each other again."

"So were your parents happy?"

"Let me just say the romance books are wrong. My mom ended up resenting my dad, who was just a repairman for the gas company, and she started drinking, and now you're into an Oprah's Book Club pick." She reaches for my hand. "I don't talk about it because it wasn't happy."

"You don't talk to them either."

"I don't even know if they're still alive. When I left home, I left for good."

That's cold.

"How old were you?"

"Sixteen."

I suck in my breath.

She laughs. "Now you know why I didn't tell you!" She slides an arm behind my shoulder and squeezes. "I know our life is crazy, but I'm trying not to make the same mistakes my parents did. Especially my mom. I'd rather it be just us, than us with the wrong guy."

"I kinda get that."

"And life on the road's not so bad. Is it?"

"It could be worse."

Her cell phone rings. She hops up and walks back to the beach fencing and the sea grass. She closes one ear with her fingertip. Her head nods over and over.

When she returns, she looks so clear and happy. "I was just filling Jeremy in on what we've seen today. He says we may need to use that inn back there—" she jerks a thumb over her shoulder to an old colonial house, a popular B and B—"to shoot a couple of scenes with Tom and Daisy and Jordon Baker and Nick and all them. There aren't any houses on Toledo or Ocracoke like that."

And I'm tired of it. It's all I can take. The untruth falls on me like a downpour only made possible by special effects, and I can no longer deny the humid weight of her lies.

I stand to my feet. "You're lying, Mom. You know, I know something's very, very wrong. I know you're scared of something. I know better than to ask what it is. But can we at least stop the pretense?"

I walk back to the inn, winding down the quaint little streets of a waterfront village where kids go to school. People are making supper and getting their things together to go visit friends, and among them I walk, a girl nobody sees.

When Charley returns, quietly laying the phone on her nightstand, I say, "Let's just go to the RV park next time we need to run away. This hurts too much."

"I'm sorry."

"I know. Will I ever know the truth?"

"Someday, when I think you can handle it."

"Does this have anything to do with my father?"

She sits down on the edge of the bed. "No, Scotty. It doesn't."

And I can't tell if she's lying or not.

I walk over to my backpack and pull out *The Great Gatsby*.

"Do you like F. Scott Fitzgerald?" she asks.

"He's my favorite."

And for a reason only Charley knows, she begins to cry. Though I travel with her all over the country, accompany her to some pretty crazy shoots with some pretty crazy people, eat her yucky food and sleep in her hippie camper, I cannot go where she is now.

She's never read Fitzgerald in her life.

I tuck the book under my arm and head for the sun porch. I'm not going to blog today. Everything and everybody else seems just a little silly right now.

Eight hours later

My phone beeps at ten thirty. Charley's been asleep for a couple of hours. We rallied and ate a nice dinner together on the windy beach. Veggie sandwiches on pita bread, soy chips with fake sour cream and onion flavoring, organic juice.

It's Seth.

When r u coming back?
Tomorrow afternoon.
Having fun w ur mom?
It's ok. Are you bored?
Completely out of my head going nuts.
Sorry. See ya later.
Bye.

Hollywood Nobody: April 12

Hello there, Nobodies. Went away for the weekend with the mom, got a little sand between the toes. Life is good.

Today's Gloat: Karissa Bonano sweats like a boxer. I kid you not. She was out jogging this morning, and she ran by where I was sitting in town, and you should have seen her shirt. I may be saying this because I'm a little catty, yes, but I'm also saying it because there are a lot of people out here who are just like her. So sweat away, my friends!

Today's Seth Haas Report: Saw him here at B-Listers. How they got that picture of him I don't know, but he's way cuter in person and never wears that kind of techno-disco-Europe shirt that I've ever seen!

Today's Kudo: Annette Bening left today. I chatted with her for a few minutes when she saw me crocheting in my lawn chair. I didn't ask what Warren Beatty is really like because she's probably sick of that question, but I did ask her how her children are and she smiled and said fine.

She has four children. One my age. She asked how old I was and I told her. A tenderness crinkled up her glorious eyes. Warren Beatty said once that he married her because she was the happiest person he had ever met. At least that's what I heard.

Today's Violette Dillinger Report: See her performance in NYC here. I'm telling you, she's the one to watch. Rumor has it she has a boyfriend from the hometown. What will happen to Mr. Boyfriend when the Violette hits it big? Will he go the way of most, or does Ms. Dillinger have what it takes to stay loyal?

Later!

Comments:

Hi, Nobody! It's me, Violette Dillinger. Thanks for talking about me here on your blog. I hope not to disappoint. Today's pop stars drive me crazy too. Call me the antidote to skanky singers. And I love my boyfriend, Ryan! Kisses out to you, babe!—Violette, 2:42 p.m.

Welcome, Violette! Thanks for stopping by. We'll keep the light on for you here on Hollywood Nobody.—hnobody, 4:45 p.m.

Whoa. Very cool of you to drop by!—hollywoodjunkie, 4:48 p.m.

I loved your song on the video!—babybaby, 9:57 p.m.

Don't any of you people have anything better to do than to hang around blogs all day? I found this site by accident, researching for school. Get a life!—Havealife, 11:32 p.m.

Oh, brother.—hnobody, 11:58 p.m.

Later

Seth and I meet for coffee at Ten Clams.

"So what was it like to work with Bening?" I ask.

"Hilarious. There's this scene where Karissa and I are caught making out by Annette, who's Daisy's mother in the movie. She's an acting teacher, and she starts yelling at Karissa, 'That's wrong! You're doing it all wrong!'"

"Sounds cute." Can't possibly imagine how that fits in with *Gatsby*.

"After the take, she says to Karissa and me, 'If it was real life and I caught my daughter sticking her tongue down a guy's throat like that, I'd ground her for a month! And no Starbucks!'"

"Kissing Karissa Bonano, eh?"

"Hey, it's my job."

"Is it kinda weird, though? Kissing girls like that?"

Joy sets down our coffee. "You guys must have the nerve endings of a Mack truck. How do you consume this much coffee in a day? Do you ever sleep?"

"Oh, yeah," I say. "Like a fat guy in the sun."

"Me too," Seth says.

"All right, then. Have at it."

Seth leans forward. "Hey, I got a call from my mom. My folks are coming down Saturday. Wanna eat with us?"

"Sure."

He pokes my shoulder. "You can get cheese." And wiggles his eyebrows.

"Don't change the subject. We were talking about Karissa Bonano and you being all in her face."

"It's my job."

"But really now. Was she a good kisser?"

"Well, yeah. But it was just a job. Man, Scotty."

Oooh-oooh. A little defensive, are we?

I look at the watch hanging from my backpack. Found it yesterday at a junk shop in Virginia before Charley and I hit the road. You have to wind it, just like my wristwatch, and the gold tone is peeling off the elasticized band, but it's great for hanging off your backpack. And the face is lavender.

Joy heads over. "Reinforcements are in. Ready?"

"Definitely!"

"I'll just go hang up my apron."

I turn to Seth. "I gotta go! I'm heading over to Joy's for a tutoring session."

"Geometry? Without me?"

"No. Sewing! She's going to teach me how to sew. I figure I can count this as an art credit, right?"

"Sounds good to me. Be good."

Like I have any other choice.

An hour later

I pull fabric out of the machine. Joy walks into the dining room where we've set up. She wipes her nose with a Kleenex.

"Are you okay?"

"Nope."

She gathers her beige hair back into two silky ponytails on

the top of her head.

"What's the matter?"

"Just opened the mail." She holds up a piece of paper. "See?"

I quickly scan it. Her mortgage is about to go into foreclosure. "What's the least amount you have to pay to keep this from happening?"

"Two thousand dollars." Huge sigh. "This place was totally paid off, but I needed the loan just to keep surviving."

"I'm going to talk to Jeremy."

"Your director friend?"

"Yeah, I mentioned you to my mom, and she said Ms. Burrell is swamped with wardrobe alterations. There are a lot of party scenes in the movie. I'll bet he'll pay you up front for the rest of the shoot. At least if I ask him I think he will." I skip down the steps and get back on my scooter. "I'll be back in a little while!"

Later that day

So back in ancient times, kings would call subjects before them for an audience, or the audience had to be requested and given the king's approval in advance. You couldn't just show up outside the throne room and say, "Hey, yeah, uh, could you tell Ratarchatusaxes that Bill's here and yeah, I can wait a little bit. No prob."

I think there's a Bible story that has something to do with that, but I'm not all that well-versed on the book myself, which is highly detrimental if you love literature like I do. I'm sure I'm missing all sorts of allusions and themes. I'm just sayin'.

Jeremy's pretty much the same way when he's working. It's like this: once everything has wrapped up, Jeremy, Charley and I, and a couple people in the inner circle of Wrenched Away Productions regroup and head somewhere for a couple of days. Jeremy's relaxed and buying drinks and is very much like an uncle.

When we're on location, though? Oh my gosh, just stay away. He gets all artsy and hyperfocused and yeah, it's probably not an act, but it feels a little cliché all the same. He's cordial but grim. And this time, he even came and told me to stay away, no offense and all.

Needless to say, I'm feeling a little queasy right now.

So when I stand behind him as he's reviewing the dailies from a few days ago, I don't know whether to clear my throat, tap him on the shoulder, or just say, "Hello, Jeremy."

I opt for the throat clearing.

He turns. "Scotty?"

"Yeah."

"What is it, kid?"

"I need you to hire an island lady to help Ms. Burrell in wardrobe. Two thousand dollars up front and she'll work for the rest of the shoot. I've never once asked you for a thing or ever complained to you about my sorry life and your part in it."

He swivels in his seat, eyes gone wider than usual. "You okay?"

"Fine. Just on a mission."

"What'll happen if this lady doesn't get the job?"

I tell him the consequences.

"Tell her she can start tomorrow." He reaches into the pocket of his moth-bitten tweed jacket, his trademark garment along with the cowboy hat and boots, and pulls out a checkbook. He signs it and hands it to me. "Fill it in yourself." He swivels back around. "Okay, Geo, let's get back to it."

I turn to leave.

"And kid!" he yells. "Don't ever do that again."

"Right, Jeremy. I'm always interrupting you."

Geo says, "Teenagers."

"No kidding." Jeremy.

I smile.

I think this is the way girls get things out of their dads. I really do.

Joy and I grab hands and dance around her living room to "Back in the High Life." Afterward, she pours some chips in a bowl, opens a couple of Cokes, and we sit on her back porch and watch the boats go by. "We can get back to sewing in a little while, Scotty. But right now, when the fishing boats are coming in, is the best time of the day."

"There's something about coming and going, isn't there? Out and back again from the same place, over and over."

"Yes." A hitherto unseen cat jumps up into her lap, orange tabby with harvest-moon eyes. "It's why I've got to stay here. We always came back here, Scotty. This place never went away."

I confide in her. I don't know what leads me to tell her about my life on the road and how I can find no place to lay my head.

"I'm sorry," she says. "It sounds like your mom is doing the best she can with the hand life has dealt."

"Whatever that hand even is."

"It sounds like something weird is going on. I have to admit it."

"I just hope it's not dangerous."

She waves a hand. "Oh, I wouldn't worry about that! That sounds a little too much like a movie." And she laughs at her own joke. But I watch her arms tighten around her cat as she pulls him in close to her heart, like he's a baby or something.

"Why don't you want to be a designer anymore?" I pop a chip into my mouth.

"Probably the design industry and the movie industry have a lot in common. You're so 'out there,' constantly being judged. I mean, when you're creative and people don't like what you've done, they might as well say they don't like you."

"That makes some people get a little nuts." I think of Maverick jumping the couch. And he'll never be Maverick again after that!

"It's hard. So when my husband left me—his name was Luke—I had to do some serious thinking. You see—" she cleared her throat—"I was pregnant when he left. He didn't know it. And I never told him."

"But—"

"Where's the baby?"

I nod.

"He died when he was three days old."

I knew there was more to the story. But why does it have to be so painful?

"So that's why you left. Really. Right?"

"Yeah." Her eyes glaze with tears. "He was beautiful, Scotty. I named him Benjamin. He had a heart defect. He died in my arms. I knew it was coming. I came to Toledo to heal. It just hasn't happened yet."

She sets down the cat, a cat I'm sure she wishes a thousand times a day was her son, live and warm, and pulls her feet up onto the chair. She hugs her knees. "I miss design. But I just can't go back. I'm not strong enough and I don't know if I ever will be."

"You hide the pain well."

"I learned how to act up there."

"I'm sure. Your work was beautiful."

Her brows raise.

I nod. "I looked you up on the Internet when Bob and Doris told me about you. I can't believe you actually designed gowns for Goldie Hawn and Geena Davis!"

"I was just about to make it really big."

"It must have been hard to leave it all."

"Uh-huh. I'm not saying other people can't do it. Rise to the challenge amid the pain."

"Is it better here?"

"I thought it would be. But this has brought its own brand of stress. I don't know if the loneliness is better or worse."

It always seems better everywhere except where your feet are standing.

Tuesday, April 13

I tug on my vintage bathing suit. The original tag still dangling from the armpit assures me it wasn't on somebody's body and all these years later the . . . well, that's just too gross to think about.

It's black. Boy-cut legs. Halter top. Very Marilyn Monroe without the D cups.

I wrap one of Charley's old sarongs around my hips, throw in a sweatshirt, sling my backpack over my shoulder, and before I head to the beach with F. Scott Fitzgerald and *Gatsby*, I check my e-mail one more time.

Oh, something's coming in! I love, love, love e-mail.

It's from Bob and Doris. Charley would kill me if she knew how many people I e-mail.

Click to open.

Hello, Sweet Scotty!
We just wanted to say hi and see if you looked up our niece Joy. We'll be in Kansas City tomorrow to stay with our friends Douglas and Katherine. He's a minister, you know.
So do write us back and let us know how everything is going for you and your mother! Bob sends his love as do I!
Sincerely,
Doris

I click reply.

Hi, Miss Doris!
I met Joy and she's so great! She really needed the encouragement like you said and has fallen on some hard times. Ocracoke isn't exactly a thriving metropolis. So anyway, we were able to get her work with the wardrobe mistress of the film, and that should keep the mortgage company from foreclosing on her house loan for now.
As for me, I'm doing fine. Joy's helping me learn geometry. We had a lesson yesterday as well as in sewing too.
It's all very good.

Tell Mr. Bob I said hi and you guys be safe out there on
the road!
Love ya!
Scotty
P.S. Do you know anything about tent meetings? Have
you ever been to one? They're having one here on the
island next weekend and I was wondering if I should go
or if it's a really creeped-out sort of thing.

Ten minutes later

On my way to the beach I pass Charley, who's rushing from the
set. "I forgot my spray oil! That corn looks drier than a fifty-year-
old wig."

"I'll be reading on the beach!" I yell to her back.

And continue on.

"Right on!" she hollers. "Stay close!"

Wow, she must be preoccupied. She didn't yell at me for going
on the beach. Things really must be heating up over there on the
set.

Seth jogs over wearing an emo getup. Yeah, he's *so* emo. He
must be a great actor to play one of those annoying creatures, and
I'm not sad to miss high school when I think about them. But
Gatsby emo? Are you kidding me? And so much for it being set
in the Depression era!

"Hey, Scotty! You going to the beach?"

"Yep." I hold up the book.

Karissa Bonano is on his heels. She swaggers to join us, wearing a bikini. Yeah, I know. "Hey."

I nod, thanking whatever God is up there that I put my wrap and a sweatshirt on over my suit. It's hardly bikini weather, and I know it's just for the shoot, but, she still looks a little silly standing there in sixty-five degree weather in a two piece.

She slips a goose-pimpled arm through Seth's. Hardly sexy. "Jeremy's calling. And you know what we're doing in this scene."

Seth rolls his eyes, not that she can see this as she lays her head against his upper arm.

"Don't tell me Jeremy's putting on screen what Fitzerald kept discreet!"

"'Fraid so." Seth shakes his head.

I turn toward the beach and Karissa says, "What's she talking about?"

One point for me.

Spreading the blanket on the deserted sand, I fume a little bit. She's so stinkin' cute! Why do certain cute girls in the world have to ruin it for everybody else?

Gatsby can wait. Elaine can't.

I write and write and write.

And you know what? I feel better. Karissa doesn't change a thing. Those girls never do until we give them permission.

Besides, I have an ethnic face, an Irish face! Maybe that's from my dad.

Later that night

Jay Gatsby, played by Robert Redford in the seventies (and was he gorgeous or what?), threw fabulous parties until he got what he wanted. One thing I haven't missed out on in my lifetime is parties. There's a party Friday night, and I'm thinking I'll head on over there for a little while before it heats up and people start acting all End of the Roman Empire on me. But until then.

Dear Elaine,

Charley made another one of her weird calls. I heard her say, "How far away is he?" Who's *he*? I swear it must be my father. But what is it that Charley doesn't want him to find out? Does he know about me?

Or maybe she committed some crime!

Oh my gosh! Maybe she was with one of those liberation groups back in the day and she killed somebody or something. Like the Patti Hearst thing, where she was drugged and brainwashed and then robbed banks! Maybe it's a crime with no statute of limitations, so that's why we're always flying under the radar.

If she doesn't give it up soon, I don't know what I'll do. Maybe I could threaten something. Starve myself? Leave a note and disappear? I wouldn't go far, really, I'd stay close enough to see her reaction, and then reappear. "Now are you ready to talk, Charley?" I'll cross my arms and throw down a frozen granite stare.

I'll be sixteen in June, so come on, Charley!

I've also decided, Elaine, that I'm a little tired of my angst these days. Hardly anybody's around to hear me anyway, and I'm getting on my own nerves.

Wednesday, April 14

Joy Overstreet brews a good cup of coffee. "I learned in Paris." In her little dining room, she sets down miniature coffee cups of espresso in front of Seth and me.

Geometry and I are getting along better than ever before. Got all of my homework assignment correct except for three problems. Okay, she only assigned seven, but I'll take what I can get. Seth kept trying to jump in and explain until I finally said, "You're confusing me."

"Fine then." But he smiled, sat back at the kitchen table, and pulled *The Star* out of his jacket pocket.

After I close my books and the coffee is finished, we decide to sit on the porch and look at the sound, the moon latticing the water as it ripples from the cool breeze blowing in off the ocean to the east.

"Does your mom do a lot of films?" Joy asks.

"Jeremy's and a few others. Jeremy does a feature length every few years, and then he does these weird projects in-between that I think will all be adding up to something in the future. Don't ask me what. It could be anything with Jeremy."

"Have you guys known him a long time?"

"Yeah. I've always known Jeremy. She also gets work from a couple of photographers in-between, old friends from art school, but mostly we just travel around when she's not working."

"Where did they meet?" Seth asks.

"He's from Baltimore. They've known each other since the fifth grade."

Which is kinda cool now that I've said it out loud.

I turn to Joy. "So how was your first day with Ms. Burrell?"

She grips the arm of her lounger. "It's going to take some getting used to. I'm normally the one calling the shots."

"Something nobody does with Ms. Burrell."

"Right. But then we started talking about children, and do you know she has nine grandchildren?"

"No!"

"Yes. And so once I figured out the way to her heart is through her relatives, I was in."

"I'll have to remember that." Seth. "She gave me a horrible time! And she's even worse to Karissa."

Joy screws up her face. "The girl sweats worse than you do. And believe me, I know how frustrating that can be. I had a few dresses almost ruined on the runway by some of those models."

"I don't sweat much," I say.

"Well we'd better sign you up for a part then."

"I don't get to Laundromats as much as I like." Now why did I volunteer *that*? I'm glad I got that in with Seth here and all. I sit up straight and face Joy. "So I've decided to build you a Web site for your jewelry."

Joy rubs her index finger around the rim of her mug. "I really can't afford that right now, Scotty."

"I'll do it for free."

Seth stands up. "And count it as computer science?"

"You got it."

"You are a girl of many talents." He leans down and kisses me on the cheek. "Okay, sis, I gotta go. Early call. Want me to walk you back to the RV?"

"That would be good."

On the way home Seth stops. "You don't like Karissa, do you?"

"I've never really talked to her. Why?"

"I don't know. She's interested in me, I can tell. But I don't know, Scotty, I don't want to hook up with a girl for the moment, you know? And it'll end after this shoot. They mostly do, don't they?"

"I've seen it happen. Just be careful. She's pretty, but she's not an innocent, Seth. Her kind will eat a regular guy like you for lunch. Maybe you should ask your mom about her."

"Good idea."

The rhythmic sound of the ocean breaking on the shore calms me even though I can't see the waves over the dunes. "Go on ahead, Seth. I want to hang out and look at the stars."

These stars are worth seeing.

I stare into the studded black space over my head, lying down near the dunes, resting my head on my backpack. It's so big up there. Deep and restful. But it's cold. So very cold.

Thursday, April 15

Looking like some medieval woman, Charley stirs a cauldron of black beans. She hates wasting beans, and she could easily make this pot look good on screen without worrying about taste, but she simply can't bring herself to do it. Beans are her favorite food. Red beans in particular. Tonight it'll be red beans and rice for dinner, I know it.

"It's tax day." I jump down from my perch. "April 15th."

"Uh-huh."

"Did you send in our taxes?"

She faces me, large spoon in hand. "Now why do you even care about that?"

"I don't know. I'm just well informed. I know these things."

"You're too smart for your own good, Scotty." She turns back to the stove, grabs a jar of bay leaves.

"So? Did you?"

She blows out her frustration between her lips and slaps a flat lid on the large pot. "I've gotta go. Big day."

"So? Did you?"

"Scotty, not now, all right?"

All right, all right.

At least she didn't want to downright lie to me like she usually does. That's a step in the right direction.

But I search for the next corner to back her into. Maybe I can wear her down! That's it. I've been too polite. I'm going to find out what's going on, bit by bit.

Hollywood Nobody: April 15

Today's Rave: Designers are donating stars' dresses from awards ceremonies and festivals for charity. Online. Visit the website <u>here</u>. The cool thing? You can actually find out what size these people are! Pamela Anderson's a size four. Now, I thought everybody was a zero these days. Good for her. Laura Linney? Size six. But the prize goes to Geena Davis. Yes, she's tall and masterful. And the gown she wore to the Golden Globes was a stunning size ten! Love the dress. Love her figure. Love everything about her.

Today's Seth Tidbit: He played football and was not a drama geek. Yes, he does have that little bit of All-American hero about him, but still. Football? We'll forgive him, though, Nobodies.

Today's Rant: Old Hollywood Families. As classy as the parents and grandparents were, the new stock, as evidenced by Karissa Bonano, could take a lesson from their home fronts. Take Paris Hilton for example too. All that classy money, but there she went swaying her rear end around a car with a soapy sponge for a hamburger (yuck), once again proving the point that just because a girl's rich does not mean she has class.

Today's Surprise: This blog has begun to get subscriptions. We're up to sixty-five members! Leave your comments folks, and join in on the fun.

Today's Quote: "Hollywood people are filled with guilt: white guilt, liberal guilt, money guilt. They feel bad that they're so rich, they feel they don't work that much for all that money—and they don't, for the amount of money they make." Drew Carey

Later!

Comments:

I'd like to try me a little some of that guilt!—hollywood-junkie, 7:09 p.m.

And then when they start complaining about the paparazzi, I'm like, come on! With the money you're making?—get_real, 7:48 p.m.

This is the lamest Hollywood blog there is. You're so squeaky clean, why bother?—perezfan, 8:45 p.m.

Later

Tomorrow is the big party for the cast and crew. I stuff as much of my clothing as I can into a trash bag and zip over to Joy's house. Going through my stuff is the last thing she'll feel like doing this evening, especially after a long day with Ms. Burrell, who's started a romance with the new cinematographer. Jeremy's old cinematographer took up with a girl from Belize and we haven't seen him in eight months. I like Geo better anyway. He reminds me of a chicken in a way. White feathery hair, a barrel chest, skinny legs, and jowls that vibrate when he snaps his gum. He seems about to invite you over for homemade vegetable soup and pumpkin bread at a moment's notice.

Joy swings the door wide before I can knock. "I heard your scooter. Come on in. What do you have with you?"

"My clothes."

Her brows raise. "Really? You do have a sense of style about you that I like."

"I'm really unsure about what to wear for the beach party tomorrow night. It's supposed to be chilly, but that's fine as I wasn't planning on going all Hawaiian or anything."

We head back to her workroom via the kitchen, where she grabs me a Coke and herself a diet Sprite. Her frizzy hair, tied back in pigtails, looks like beige shower puffs.

"Okay, let's spread things out on the table. So obviously you like vintage and it's definitely working for you. But you tend to cut yourself in half right at the waist, and I think a longer line would really work."

In other words, I'm a little chunky around the middle.

"Hey, whatever you say. I was hoping we could finish up the dress we've been working on, but that might be too fancy anyway."

"It is. You don't want to ever look like you're trying too hard. Are you?"

"Am I what?"

"Trying too hard?"

"About what?"

"About *who* is more like it."

"Seth?"

She spreads out my new tulle prom dress, fingering the netting with care. "This is really pretty, Scotty. Yes, Seth. Who else?"

"Is it obvious? I'm really trying hard not to make it obvious."

"Only to me, I think. I had a crush on my religion teacher back in seventh grade. He was fresh out of Bible college and I thought he was gorgeous. And he was." She folds the bodice of the dress underneath the skirt. "I've never told anybody that before!" and she laughs.

"What are you doing?"

"Well, I'm thinking we can make this two pieces and you'll get so much more wear out of it. A nice big tulle skirt to wear with other shirts, a skinny tank or a T, and then this bodice you can wear with jeans or capris. I'll add some trim to the bottom so it'll rest at your hips and not your waist. What do you think? It would expand things for you. I know your space in that camper is limited."

"Can you do that?"

She *pffs*. "Oh sure. It'll only take me a few minutes. Now. What do you think if we pair the bodice with this pair of pants?"

"I hate those things. I don't know why I even brought them."

"Watch this." She takes the old jeans, which are totally too pegged, and says, "Try them on so I can measure a hem. I'm going to cut them off and make a skirt out of them."

"You're amazing."

"Yeah, I like to think that sometimes."

She sews away and gives me advice on Seth that I'd already given myself, how at my age it's okay to have these crushes but he's a grown man—well, sort of—and it would blow the friendship to make any sort of advance as he sees me as a kid, which yes, I knew, but who wants to really think of it that way?

"And honestly, Scotty, if a guy his age did like you, wouldn't you wonder what's wrong with him?"

Oh. Yeah. "That's true!"

"See?"

Why can't I have these kind of talks with Charley?

An hour later, the bodice is plucked from its skirt which she finished off with a grosgrain waistband and a zipper. The jeans are now a flowing skirt, flared by insets of coordinating fabric that

Joy "just happened to have on hand" and sewed into the seams. I know it's designer silk and hideously expensive.

I don't pray very much, but I send up a prayer that God will work things out for Joy. She's too nice to struggle for the rest of her life.

She waves me off, tears in her eyes.

Friday, April 16

Joy offered to help me get ready for the party. A real fashion designer come to my aid! Normally I don't even want to be near these creepy social gatherings, but with Seth going, Charley didn't have to work too hard to convince me. This surprised her because of previous cast-crew party disasters:

1. The time I fell asleep in Ethan Hawke's trailer and didn't know it. I was four. He wasn't impressed by my cuteness.

2. Accidentally rounding a corner and skidding into a cocaine fest at the age of ten. The fact that I yelled at them for being stupid didn't help matters any, and thank goodness it was near the end of the shoot.

3. Not knowing the punch was, well, "punched" and getting sicker than I could have imagined, and did that ever cure me of thinking that falling-down-drunk is anything more than falling-down-moronic. That sure is one thing my unconventional education spares me from—watching kids make idiots out of themselves.

So I gather my makeup/hair-stuff bag, a sixties bowling bag

in tooled leather labeled "Jack Wood." I don't know who Jack Wood is, but I like his bowling bag. Picked it up in Minnesota for $4.36.

I hop aboard my scooter and figure I'll head to the beach first, lay out just enough to make my face rosy, and finish up my report on the lighthouses here on the Outer Banks. Hopefully Charley will take me up to Cape Hatteras and Currituck Beach Light before we ship out of this place. I need some pictures for the finishing touches on my scrapbook pages.

You know, I could complain a lot about my schooling, but I've sure learned to work in obscurity, be a self-starter. Charley barely even looks over my work, and so I file it away dutifully in hopes that somebody someday will look at it and deem me worthy of their institution of higher learning. I suspect, however, Charley will try to talk me out of college.

Ya think?

I fire up the scooter and head to the beach. I've wanted to be a lot of things so far: a doctor, a chef, a food stylist (that lasted about fifteen seconds), a journalist, a director, a cameraman, a costume designer, an accountant (settle down somewhere, be happy and stable), a fire eater (travel even more than I do now), and a dog trainer.

But right now, I'm wondering what would suit me. I love cheese. Maybe I can become an artisan cheese maker. Buy a farm in Wisconsin, raise cute little goats.

Zooming by Jeremy's trailer (he always bunks down on the outskirts of the shoot, has this Airstream he's been towing around for years) I hear my name called from inside.

"Scotty!" He draws out the "eeeeeeee"! And I turn into his lot.

"Come on in, kid! I have a question to ask you."

"Okay."

I step down, remove my helmet, and lean the scooter against the trailer.

"So what's up?"

My eyes adjust to the innards of his tin can. Now I call the Y a tin can, but that's metaphorically speaking. This looks like a tin can. I love it. So retro. He sits on a leather couch stamped with a cheetah design; his feet, swaddled in those old cowboy boots, rest on an asymmetrically triangular coffee table. At the other end a single bed hugs the wall, and small kitchen appliances divide the space.

"Hey, kiddo. Have a seat. Where you off to?"

"The beach, to study. Why aren't you on the set?"

"We had a little mishap. One of the twins broke a tooth. She's at the dentist now. Her mother's having a fit, yammering on and on about how there can't possibly be a good dentist out here in no-man's land."

"Did she say that? 'Out here in no-man's land?' Like the Billy Joel song?"

"Scout's honor." He held up three fingers. Hard to imagine Jeremy as a Boy Scout. "So, kiddo, tell me about this seamstress lady. Joy Overstreet. I like to know where my charity goes."

I tell him everything I know, including her escape from New York and the death of her newborn son. Jeremy misted over, as well he should. "After I finish my schoolwork, I'm headed over to her house. She's going to help me get ready for the party."

"Yeah? She's a nice gal then, eh?"

"Most definitely."

"Ms. Burrell likes her. Says Joy's a better sewer and designer than she is."

"She was almost big in New York, Jeremy." I sit next to him on the couch, lean forward and pick up a papier-mâché star from the coffee table. He made it in college one year for a tree-topper and can't get rid of it.

He raises his dark, bushy brows. "Almost? That doesn't count for much these days."

"Neither does talent."

"You got that right, kid. I like her. She's pretty, in a real natural way. Like the way she's got those . . . hips. Hips. I haven't seen a real pair of them in years."

"You obviously don't get around much. Have you talked to her?"

"Some. Real nice. Just wanted your take on her."

"Why?"

He shrugs.

So, off to the beach now. For real.

I spread out my blanket and lay on my stomach, my head facing the breakers. The ocean shines the dark blue of a newborn baby's eyes, and a piercing sun coats the skin of the waters. Probably somewhat like the view Gatsby would have had during a spring day on West Egg.

Now, of course, having been around drama all of my life, I think Gatsby was a big phony. I think he was definitely tied up with the mob. I think he never did go to an Ivy League school. He was nothing but a grown-up playing dress-up, as evidenced by his simple father at the end. Wait—was that at the end of the movie or the book? It's all blurring!

If Fitzgerald thought the Jazz Age an era of excess, he would have had a field day with today's Hollywood! Too bad he died too soon.

So I settle in, read until the part they visit Myrtle's house for the first time. I can't stand that Myrtle! I reach into my backpack for a cheese sandwich. I smuggled in more cheese last night, this time going for the Tofutti container. Charley hates Tofutti.

Time for geometry.

The afternoon drags on. I try to concentrate, but I keep thinking about Jeremy. Is he really interested in Joy? And how will that make Charley feel? Well, she won't hear it from me. And why in the world would he need my take on it all? I mean, really?

Dear Elaine,

If Jeremy really was my dad, I'd be pretty mad at him for keeping it from me all these years. There's no good reason that I can think of to do that to your daughter.

But why else would he care what I think about Joy?

And yet, if Jeremy really was my dad, I'd finally have somebody to be mad at. And after we got all of that out of the way, we'd go out for a 16-inch pizza, extra cheese, and I'd visit him at the cheetah Airstream and we'd watch obscure old movies while he called me kiddo. As in you're-my-kid kiddo.

Five minutes later

Okay, I'm done with all that fantastical dreck. I head over to Joy's. She's going to be excited. Her website is looking great. The header is art nouveau, very feminine, yet with that "good art" feel to it. Just like her necklaces.

I open my laptop and show her. She hugs me. "When can it go live?"

"As soon as you give me the pictures and descriptions. Also, have you thought about contacting your friends from the design world? Maybe you could design down here. Jewelry, not clothing."

"Maybe." She doesn't look too certain. Is there another reason she doesn't want to go back to New York, not even virtually?

Joy stands up. "Okay, an hour-and-a-half left until the party. Hop in the shower—" I stoop over to pick up my backpack—"and I'll get the straightening iron heating up."

I freeze, bent double. "The straightening iron?"

"Sure! You want to make a statement right?"

How do I tell her this?

"Joy? How many straightening irons have probably been sold in the last five years?"

"Lots."

I stand up. "So what statement would I be making by straightening my hair?"

"Okay, I get it. An updo then?"

"Now you're talking. Or something retro, like Jordon Baker in *The Great Gatsby*."

"Oh, Lois Chiles. I loved her in *The Way We Were*."

"Me too. Now she was a real beauty."

"Okay, but I'm still going to have to use a straightening iron, Scotty, and then put in those bends and waves."

"That's fine. As long as I don't look all Hollywood. Current Hollywood, I mean."

"You'll be gorgeous. Old Hollywood. Lots of glamour."

I highly doubt that. However, I'm willing to let her give it her best shot.

A little later

The shower was so glorious, the stall so large and roomy, I just twirled around in it while the warm water spilled over my head. I guess one of the perks of my life is that I don't *ever* take the mundane for granted.

But now, sitting at the kitchen table having my hair straightened, wouldn't you know it, Joy starts asking me about Jeremy. "So you've known him for years, right, Scotty?"

"Yep. Pretty much all my life."

"He seems eccentric, but nice."

"That describes Jeremy. Are you interested in him?"

"The question is, is he interested in me?"

"Do you want him to be?"

She places a hand on top of my head, holding it upright as she pulls with the straightening iron. "I don't know. I don't know if I'm ready for all that. Maybe it's too soon."

"That's certainly something to consider." I sure don't want to encourage a date between Joy and my maybe-father. I mean she's nice and all, but please, Jeremy's a *true* genius.

She shrugs. "It's just something to think about, I guess. I feel so isolated down here and I can't help wondering if I'm even remotely an attractive woman anymore."

Okay, so I feel bad about the true-genius thing.

"Well, I think you're gorgeous." I turn to face her and she swings the iron out of my way. "Were you bulimic or something up there?"

"No!" She sets down the iron. "Yes. Yes, I was. How did you know?"

"I have this weird sense for stuff, having observed people from the outskirts for so long. It's no wonder you can't go back. Do you think I'm fat, Joy?"

"Of course not! But I'm a lot bigger than you are."

"Not much. So maybe you should go ahead and give Jeremy one of those womanly signs you're interested."

Did I really just say that? Crap!

She places her hands on her hips. "Maybe you're right."

I wonder if she was bulimic and starved herself, if that had something to do with Benjamin's death. But of course, I don't ask. There's enough grief in this world without always getting into whose fault it is.

Two hours later

I'm totally overdressed.

I look like I'm ready for a night at the Oscars (well, maybe a night at the Ricks or the Bobs would describe it a little better) and everybody else is hanging out in jeans and tight little shirts showing their tight little bellies just above the low-rise waistbands of their tight little jeans.

I hate my life! Scrap that. I hate *their* lives and what they do to *my* life! Charley, Charley, Charley! Why do we have to be here?

"Scotty!" Seth shouts from a picnic table across the sand. "Over here!"

Could you just shout a little bit louder please, Seth? Could you maybe call everybody's attention to me please? Could you maybe, while you're at it, shine a spotlight on my gorgeous bodice and jean skirt that screams "Trying too hard!"?????

Could you maybe stop looking so casual and cute in those faded jeans and that T-shirt?

I hurry over as fast as I can, my sleek waves bouncing around my head. Okay, here goes. These stars think they can act? Ha! Just watch me.

"Hi, Seth. Great party, huh?"

"Ha ha." He gestures around him. "They're already halfway to wasted. Hey, meet my parents." He turns to the people sitting to his left, a real couply-couple. Real people with real cheekbones and chins. Gray streaks in the woman's hair. Crows feet and polyester on the man!

I'm in love with them already.

"These are my parents. Edie and Stephen."

Edie looks garden-artsy, if you know what I mean. She could easily be wearing a big straw hat and holding a spade. Love the loose blue skirt and man-shirt she's wearing. Espadrilles too. The lady, I'm telling you, is cool.

I shake their hands. "Nice to meet you, Mr. and Mrs. Haas."

Mrs. Haas smiles, pleasingly crooked teeth glowing in the twilight. Nice pearlish lipstick too. "Seth's told us so much about you."

"You sound like an extraordinary young woman!" Mr. Haas nods a head full of thick red hair, showing off a light sparkling of silver. Oh, freckles still loiter on the bridge of his nose. He sits like a Raggedy Andy and I love him to death, polyester slacks and all. I really do.

"Sit down with us." Seth scoots over. "You want something to eat?"

"No. I'm really not hungry. The waistband on this skirt's a little tight."

Why did I say that?

Mrs. Haas pats my hand, eyes looking into mine like the fairy godmother's must have looked into Cinderella's. "You look beautiful, honey. Much prettier than anybody here."

"I think so too," says Seth.

Yes!

"I'm getting you something to drink, Scotty." He stands up. "A real Coke?"

"Is Charley around?"

"Not yet that I can tell."

"Real Coke, then."

Seth's parents smile.

The twins walk by, take one look at my outfit, and start to giggle. Oh, please. Like I really care.

I look up by the drinks table and there stands Karissa, pushing her manufactured chest all out, holding her stomach — all size two of it — in and laying her hand on Seth's forearm.

She glances over in my direction, slips her arm through Seth's, and they walk toward me. Dear God, if you're there, help me not to do something stupid. Make those tight jeans constrict if they have any room at all and cut off her blood flow at the hips, make her twist an ankle on those high-heeled boots, make that mane of hair get blown away like a hat or something. Anything.

However, they keep on walking. No trips, no mishaps, not even one person interrupting their journey toward us. Like they're in a movie or something.

Seth introduces Karissa to his parents. They're very nice to her, but they look suspicious of her. She sits down without invitation and charms them.

I'm forgotten. Until.

She turns to me. "Scotty, right?"

"That's me."

"Seth told me he's helping you with geometry. So you're . . . *home*schooled? I've never met anybody homeschooled before. You seem normal. Well, sort of." She giggles. "No offense, but the outfit is a little over the top. Really cute though. You must have a lot of confidence." Then turns to Seth. "Ready? Let's find people our age for a little while."

Seth mouths, "Sorry Scotty," and turns away with Karissa.

We wait for his return for the next hour. I sit with his parents, answering all their questions about Hollywood and film shoots and Jeremy and do I really think Seth is going to be a big star until finally Mr. Haas says, "Guess we'll be getting back to our room. Sorry you had to hang around with people 'our age.'"

Mrs. Haas rolls her eyes. "Imagine only hanging out with people your own age? How boring."

I laugh. "Actually, you're way more interesting than most of the people around here. Especially the Karissas." No wonder Seth is such a nice guy. Too bad he let a girl like her lure him away from the real fun. I watch them mosey off, wishing.

Charley runs up to the table with the mustard costume!

What?!

"Stand up! Stand up, Scotty!" she hisses.

I climb to my feet and she jams it down over my head.

"What are you doing, Charley?"

"Don't say anything. Just walk out of here like you're an entertainer brought in for the party or something."

Yeah, right. You can have a clown, Cinderella, Barney, or a big yellow mustard.

Her cell phone rings. "Yes, I've got her. Where are you? Okay we're almost there."

Through my mustard mesh I see a burly man standing at the edge of the beach, looking at the party scene. He's a biker, obviously, tattooed and tough, his shaved head gleaming in the torchlight. Leather chaps overlay his blue jeans and his large hands rest on a heavy silver belt buckle.

We round the corner of the wardrobe trailer and the side door of a white van slides open. Charley hurries me over and helps me inside. She climbs in after me and says, "Okay, Jeremy. Let's go."

Jeremy pulls away. We drive past our campsite. The Y is gone.

"Where's the Y? What's going on?"

"We can't say, baby." Charley. "It really is for your own good not to know."

"It really is." Jeremy.

"Where are you taking me?"

"Joy's." Charley. "You're going to spend the night there. I'll be back to get you in the morning if all is clear."

"Who was that guy?"

"What guy?" Charley looks like her foot's suddenly been trapped in a bear claw.

"That big biker-looking dude. You know exactly who I'm talking about."

"Stay away from him, Scotty. He's not your friend."

"Is this who we've been running from all these years?"

Big sigh. "Yes!"

"So we are running from somebody! And in a mustard costume!"

"Stop asking questions. If you ever see that man again . . . hide! Do you hear me?"

"Yes, Charley, sheesh."

Jeremy grips the steering wheel. "Charley's got good reasons, kiddo. She really does."

Sunday, April 18

Joy griddles up a high stack of white-flour pancakes with real maple syrup for breakfast. Even Charley would approve of the syrup. I fork a big, fluffy bite into my mouth, grateful for Joy's food and her tolerance of my spending Saturday in silent fury. She didn't even get nosy. "So did Charley or Jeremy say anything about the situation?"

Joy seems relieved that I'm speaking again. "Nope. And I don't want to know about it either. I'm just glad you're safe. They called before you woke up and gave the all-clear. He's gone."

"Is the Y back in place?"

She shakes her head. "Huh?"

"Our camper."

"I don't know. But as soon as you eat, I'll drive you back over to Toledo."

"Thanks." I call Charley. The camper's on the other side of the shoot.

Fifteen minutes later I step up into the camper. Charley hops up from the dinette. "Scotty. You okay, baby?"

"Sure! Never better. I get spirited away in the night as a giant mustard, away from some guy that looks tougher than George Hamilton's skin, of course I'm fine. I'm going to church. Maybe I'll find better answers there."

"I'll fix you breakfast."

"No thanks. I already had pancakes made with store-brand white flour, non-organic butter, as in from-a-cow butter, and lots of sugary syrup. I won't even tell you what I ate Saturday."

Charley flinches.

I slam my hand down on the table. "What did you think was going to happen, Charley? You've got to tell me *someday* what's going on."

"I can't. Trust me, Scotty. I just can't."

"Yeah, we've been over it before." I yank my clothes bin out from under one of the dinette benches and pull on a corduroy skirt, a pink T-shirt, and a cardigan I got in a junk store in Kansas City for a buck fifty.

A few minutes later I'm out the door, careening in the sunshine on my scooter toward some crazy church with people who are probably even crazier than Charley. But I've got to get out of here. Out of this camper. Away from this stupid movie set. Away from my life. A life I don't even know anything about.

Fifteen minutes later

They really did set up a tent—a soaring white tent with three poles down the middle. Now I imagine this kind of affair was pretty simple in John Wesley's day. They were called camp meetings back then too, and people would set up camp for a week or more because it took so long to travel, and they'd listen to Wesley preach. He was English but became a really big deal over here. He founded Methodism. I haven't read any of his sermons yet, but I'm planning to. Can't really know about the man until I read what he said.

I slip in unnoticed. I'm extremely good at that. And I settle myself on a metal folding chair at the back right-hand corner, near the tent flap, ready for a quick exit if need be.

A band warms up on the right side of the platform up front. The music, definitely gospel, mixes a classic bluegrass twang with a more glitzy Nashville sound, with some local cornfield thrown in as well. The musicians are all dressed in black. A woman with flame-red hair saws away on an electric fiddle, lips pursed, eyebrows raised so high you wonder if she painted them on. One man, very large with those legs that seem to be screwed on at the hips, sits on a kitchen chair and plucks at a banjo. I'll bet he owns a poodle. A younger guy as skinny as the tent pole, dirty blond hair slicked back in a ponytail, strums on a guitar and his sound is very smooth, very nice. The drummer, mixed-race, I think, keeps time with a minimum of movement and seems like the type of guy that would drink Coke for breakfast. The singers, a quartet dressed in white, go over various harmonies. An African American woman, white hat perched on her head, sings lead and plays the lead. She seems to be the leader all around. The bassist is black as well, and my goodness, I can see his blue eyes from here! And I love his vintage plaid pants. The other singers are white, two women, with bleached-blond Farrah hair and lots of makeup. They could be twins except one is six inches taller than the other and I don't really think they're related. They're just doing themselves up the exact same way. And without warning they seamlessly transition from their warm up into the real-live playing.

"Hallelujah! And glory to God!" the lead singer says as the drummer taps that one-two gospel beat. "I'm Sister Lindelle and welcome to this morning's tent revival service, glory to God. We gonna welcome the Holy Spirit into our midst and praise the name of Jesus. Praise Jesus, we're going to get our praise on and worship the living God!"

The band picks up and soon the entire congregation is singing and swaying to a song I've never heard. Naturally. A few people begin running around the tent, one waving a swatch of purple lamé fabric.

It's the strangest scene I've ever been in, because nobody's an actor here, but there's this kind of meaning I can't put my finger on. And yet . . .

It's a show.

Plainly it's a show.

I take notes for the paper I'll be writing, a paper nobody will ever see.

"Hey!" a male voice shouts in my ear. I turn around.

"Mr. Haas!"

"Scoot on over, friend. Me and Edie want to join you."

"Where's Seth?"

"I don't know. He's not big on church anymore." Mrs. Haas. "But we are. So if you don't mind, we'll just sit next to you."

This is nice. This is very nice.

The preaching team gets up next. Reverend Hank and Reverend Kim Jones.

"I didn't realize Pentecostals had women preachers," I say to Mrs. Haas.

"Oh yes. We're tied to Wesley and he thought it was a fine idea."

"My mom used to be Catholic when she was little. They definitely do *not* have women priests."

And Kim begins to preach, only I soon find out she's "prophesying."

"What's that?" I whisper to Mr. Haas.

"You can find out all about it at lunch. We're taking you

out if you want."

"Most definitely."

Reverend Kim breaks into song as she prophesies and preaches, hopping up and down a little on the balls of her feet, the band playing in time to her words. Her bright orange getup sparkles and shimmers, a powerful combination against the band's outfits.

Yep. A show.

People come forward to be healed, and I wonder if healers have their own particular style. Because these people sort of hold their hands on the top of folks' heads, look up to the heavens with their eyes closed, and mutter words I've never heard before. And I've learned a little Latin on the computer. And German. And nothing they're saying sounds like it comes from either one.

I've seen some healing preachers on TV. One guy I've seen looks like he's clobbering people! But not these folks. They seem kind of soft and gentle when they're doing this. Yet there's that part inside of me that crosses its arms and says, "I bet this is all an act. I bet they're frauds like in the movies."

And then the man gets up to preach. He wears a contemporary suit, like you'd see on Sean Combs. He laughs at his own jokes, but not in that nice-guy way, and he just sort of talks through his spiel like he's done it a thousand times before. He's what I've always suspected. His words are aflame and I am going to hell, I think. I'm going to "step into eternity without Jesus."

I can't wait to get something to eat. This is all creeping me out a little.

An hour later

Ten Clams is filled to capacity, so Mr. Haas buys a loaf of bread, some ham, mustard (ugh!), cheese (yes!), chips, and Coke, and we head to the picnic area at the small municipal park near the island's more touristy beach. He makes sandwiches, and Mrs. Haas and I watch him.

"For some reason, Steve's sandwiches always taste better than mine."

"Can I have cheese on both sides of the meat?" I ask.

"Is it right to make it any other way?" he asks.

I love these people!

Mrs. Haas opens the Grandma Utz chips and tilts the cellophane bag my way. I grab a few.

"So what was Seth like as a kid?"

She slides some out as well. "Like he is now, only smaller."

"Really?"

"Yes. He's always been that nice."

"Does this whole Hollywood thing scare you, then?"

"Yes." Mrs. Haas.

"No." Mr. Haas.

I laugh. "Well, you can always call me with any questions."

Mr. Haas opens the mustard. "That's good to know. You're quite the expert, eh?" His blue eyes sparkle.

"Not really. I mean, if you're talking what I've actually *done*. But I've pretty much seen it all."

Mrs. Haas lays a hand on my arm. "That's so sad. I'm sorry you have to see this stuff. If it's what I've always imagined."

Okay. I have to reassure her now. Because, to be honest, it isn't all bad.

"It's not all bad. Yeah, I've seen more than I probably should have. I've walked in on people doing things I never should see at my age. But I've got to tell you, there are some really nice people in the film industry. The grips are usually the best, and my mom works selectively, so I've gotten to know people over the years. Ms. Burrell, for example, a costumer. She's like a crotchety grandmother to me. We're like a big, dysfunctional family.

"And some of the actors will surprise you at how nice they are." I lean forward. "It's mostly the young ones that really drive me crazy."

"Like Seth?" She smiles.

"He's the exception. Jake Gyllenhaal's pretty nice too."

"Who's he?" asks Mr. Haas.

"He's one of the young studs, honey." Mrs. Haas. "A lot of the blogs say he's gay."

I clap my hand over my mouth. "You read the Hollywood blogs?"

"How else am I going to find out about this stuff?"

"What's a blog?" Mr. Haas.

"Oh, Stephen. You're so out of touch."

"What are your favorites?" I ask. Have to find out what the public likes, right?

She lists several and then offers up her non-favorites. B-Listed and Nick Ole Richie. "They're so foul!"

"I know! My advice on those . . . *never* look after the jump."

"Honey, I already know! You've *seen* some of those pictures? Oh, dear!"

"Believe me, I'm scarred for life."

"There's a new one that talks about Seth all the time. Hollywood Nobody." She leans forward. "It's definitely somebody here at the shoot, because they know all about what's going on."

"Really?" I gasp. "I wonder who it is?"

"I don't know. But it's definitely a female. And she calls him Seth Hottie. Isn't that cute?"

"Adorable!" My voice is getting louder and louder.

And she winks at me. She knows. Darn it, Mrs. Haas knows.

"I'm not happy with Karissa either, honey. Just so you know."

"Sandwiches are done!" Mr. Haas sets them on napkins and slides them our way.

We say grace. Or rather, they say grace and I listen.

"So. What did you think of the tent meeting?" Mrs. Haas bites into her sandwich. "Good job, Stephen!"

"Well, I've got mixed emotions."

"Naturally." Mr. Haas.

"I mean, is God really all mad at people like that? What if they've never really heard all that much about Jesus? What if nobody's ever really explained and they've never been around church or anything? What if the only Christian people they've ever met are jerks? Doesn't that count for something? Or is he really so angry he doesn't take anybody's situation into account?"

"He hates sin," Mr. Haas says. "But God loves everybody, Scotty."

"That guy sure didn't make it sound like that. He made it sound like God's just mad at the world."

Mrs. Haas tells me about Jesus. And I just never knew about this side of him. She's gentle and sweet and her words ring like music somehow.

"The thing I love about Jesus so much is, he's with me

wherever I go. He's the one thing constant about my life. His love never changes."

Yeah. I could use a good dose of that.

They don't push it all on me, though, and I appreciate that. There's only so much spirituality a person can handle at one time.

Soon we're onto Seth stories. And man, if I ever need it, do I have some ammo now!

Hollywood Nobody: April 18

Hello, Nobodies! It's been a few days, but I've got some dish on Seth Haas, and did you see him in the latest issue of US? A reporter came to his current shoot and got some great pics of Seth on the beach. The boy is hot, hot, hot. More on him later.

Today's Rave: Oh my gosh! There's a reality show coming on this week called "Realer than Reality" and I'm so excited. The premise? Four people have to make a real go in a house . . . all of them on minimum wage! And how great is this? No Real World cool loft in New York. No icebox modern house with celebrities. Nobody eating yucky body parts of animals. The true drama of survival and I am all for it, Nobodies! Stay tuned for what goes on. You can find the episode descriptions and teasers here.

Today's Tidbit: Who just got plastic surgery? Her first round, folks. Take a peek after the jump.

Today's Quote: "My driving abilities from Mexico have helped me get through Hollywood." Salma Hayek

Today's Rant: Too tired! But let's just say, I'm curious about people famous for being famous. What's up with that?

Also: Violette Dillinger's debut album released today. Anybody get a copy yet? I'm in a remote location so no go. Tell us how it is!

Comments:

Got the Dillinger album this morning. The girl's amazing!—hollywoodjunkie, 3:53

Violette's vocals are really great. And her songs were totally creative. The liner notes and pictures make it seem like she's a down-to-earth person. Find a copy if you can.—newviolettefan, 4:37 p.m.

Later

I'm antsy. I shut the lid on my laptop.

Earlier I ate a piece of clandestine cheese. I blogged. I popped that zit in my ear that won't go away and repierced my third hole in my left earlobe. How could I have not realized it was closing up? It had been, what, three months since I put an earring in? I have no idea. I even visited with Jay Gatsby as long as I could, and when he wasn't enough to calm my nerves, I scrubbed down the Y's kitchen and bath because Charley decided to nap on the beach and she completely deserved to. She's been putting in the hours and now that she knows Jeremy likes Joy, she's feeling a little depressed.

And it's still only three o'clock!

More tent meeting tonight at seven. I'm meeting Mrs. Haas at ten of. Seth must have been freaking out when she had cancer because, I kid you not, she's one of the nicest ladies I've ever met. Ever. The woman used to take in foster children. I mean, who really does that sort of thing? I've never met a foster mom before. What lucky kids is all I can say. It's hard to imagine losing someone so cool.

I mean, Charley's *not* cool and I can't imagine losing her either. I'm hard on my mother. Too hard. But I hate this shiftless life on the road.

So I've got to get out of this tin-can home. Right now. I climb on my scooter and head for Ocracoke to stay clear of Charley. I bought a can of squirt cheese, which she'll supernaturally know is in my backpack. I also packed a blanket, my iPod, and my cell phone. I don't want words now. I think I just want to listen to music and fall asleep. That's one way to get a boring afternoon out of the way.

As I spread out the blanket near the lighthouse—a squat, white cone with a black bonnet lantern—the breeze exhales a spring warmth on my face. Yet April is evidenced by the fact I'm still comfortable in jeans and Charley's old fisherman's sweater. A sunshine sweetness cushions the air, and the rustle of the sea oats makes me feel like I'm with someone nice.

Lying back, I close my eyes against the sharp sunlight; I plant my earbuds into my ears and turn on some Miles Davis. The Quintet. Yep, this is really nice. To just lie here. To just be.

Even later

The music ends. My phone beeps. I sit up.

Drat. I didn't want to read anything. But who can resist a text message, right?

From Seth: Where r u? i've been looking for u for 3 hours!

Three hours?! Oh my gosh, it's almost six o'clock!

Me: On the beach at Ocracoke. Fell asleep. Will be back soon. You're pretty good at disappearing yourself.

Seth: Karissa needed to talk.

Oh yeah, right. Little Miss Perfect and all.

Me: I'm meeting your mom at tent meeting. I'd better go home and get ready. See you later.

There. Let him sit on that. Karissa needing a confidante?

Seth: ok. maybe we can have cheese tomorrow.

I don't return a text. I've gotta go. And he didn't mention how mean Karissa was to me, did he?

About an hour later

Mrs. Haas wears a long denim skirt with arsty flowers painted on it. Not appliquéd craft-store flowers. Mammoth platters of petals, Georgia O'Keefe flowers.

I love Georgia O'Keefe, by the way. She was just crazy! Cool hat too.

Mrs. Haas waves as I chain up my scooter. "Scotty! I've saved us seats near the front!"

Oh great.

Still. She's so nice, I don't really mind. And have you ever noticed how that is? When people are really kind, you just don't seem to mind when they do or say things that make you a little uncomfortable, do you?

She tucks her arm through mine and leads me up the aisle.

"Where's Mr. Haas?"

"He's spending time with Seth. I think they're going surf fishing or something."

"With Karissa?"

"Definitely not!" She laughs.

Good.

She grabs my hand as we sit on the side-by-side metal folding chairs. The band begins warming up. I like that singing lady with the dark honey skin. She nods in recognition, smiles right into my eyes and belts out the beginning of a happy song.

Eventually, the evangelists take over the platform and start yelling again. Why are they yelling at me? That's what I want to know. What did I ever do to deserve this?

Nah, I kinda get it. Old-school preaching and all. But you know, it's just a little "out there" when you're watching it live and not on television.

Two hours later

Mrs. Haas and I dig into grilled cheese sandwiches and fries at Ten Clams.

"So what did you think of the meeting?" She dips a fry into ranch dressing. See. I told you she was cool.

"Kinda weird. I've only been to church a few times."

"I can see where that would have been strange then."

"But not totally. I mean, I've grown up around movie sets. Hardly a reality-based atmosphere."

"True."

"I've learned to look for the hidden meaning under all the shine."

"Hmm."

I take a bite of my sandwich. Joy is cooking tonight. It's the perfect grilled cheese—just the right amount of buttery crisp on the outside, the perfect gooey melt on the inside. Seriously, is there anything better?

"So what was your take on it all, then?" she asks. "Now that you're an experienced tent-meeting goer."

"I don't know. I researched the old Wesleyan tent meetings before I went, so I was expecting something a lot different. The singing was great. Hated the preaching. The healing was cool, but I wonder whether it was real."

"You have anything needing to be healed?"

"Nothing God can help me with, Mrs. Haas."

"Oh, honey. What is it?"

But I shake my head. I can't tell her about my need for a father. A dad. It's so . . . so cliché. Like a typical movie with a teen queen.

Monday, April 19

I'm definitely a little low on art credits, so when Joy asked me to come over and make jewelry, I didn't have to think. Really, I mean: hang around the Y, or string amethyst and garnet onto funky wire and tiger tail? Hardly a grueling decision.

Truth is, as we sit and string, I have to admit there's something really wonderful about Joy. It's easy to see why the fashion industry literally consumed her, flesh and bone. Some people are too gentle for that much pressure.

She'll reach out with delight and say, "Oh! Look at these lines on this malachite!" or "Jasper never stops surprising me."

I reach for one of the nachos she made me for lunch. I so do not have a problem with eating. Seth is right. I'm not skinny, but I'm not fat. I'm fine. I'm healthy. I'm—

Robust.

Yes. Robust. Which means, strong, healthy, and vigorous.

So she's totally smitten with Jeremy, who's apparently over at the costume trailer more than Ms. Burrell thinks he should be, and inundates me with questions.

How old? Fifty-six.

Graduate from college? Yep, the Maryland Institute of Art.

"Wow, great school!

Favorite color? Maroon.

Favorite food? Steamed crabs.

Kids? Hello. Never married.

"Uh, you're kidding. Right, Scotty?"

"Hey, I have high hopes for people. What can I say?"

She shakes her head, chuckles, then exhibits a gorgeous toggle clasp that looks like a ladybug sitting on a leaf. "Fabulous or what?"

"I had no idea there was stuff like this!"

"It's fun, isn't it?" She pulls a little drawer of marcasite beads out of her organizer, one of those plastic boxes with lots of little drawers, like something on an old man's workbench, Bob's workbench if he had one in his RV, holding all sorts of little screws and nuts and bolts and whatever an old grandpa needs for his jiffy repairs around the house.

My cell phone rings. Charley.

"You've got to get back here right away! And I mean right now!"

Oh no. Not again.

"Go right to Ms. Burrell's trailer and get on that mustard suit and head to the shoot on Main."

Oh no! Not again for real! I thought I was going to be spirited away into the setting sun to get away from that fat bald guy.

"Are you serious?"

"Now, Scotty!"

I shut my phone. "I gotta go. There's a big padded mustard costume with my name on it."

"Oh, I saw that! It's awful."

So I apologize for leaving my portion of the bead mess, and I scoot on back to Toledo, the afternoon sun warming the back of my neck, and I'm so mad Seth blew me off for Karissa. Again. We could have had a nice day, lazing on the beach, reading our books.

I pull up to the trailer. Ms. Burrell already waits outside with the suit. She shoves it down over my head and points me toward the same corner I waved on before.

When I arrive, Jeremy pats my cone top. "Nobody waves better than you, kid."

"Save it for the divas, Jeremy."

"Quiet on the set!"

A couple of hours later

So she's totally kidding me, right? Who in her right mind would actually believe this stunt? At least I'm out of the mustard suit, but I'm still in town, sitting at Ten Clams, trying desperately to drink the thick strawberry milk shake the cook brought over without me even asking. His name is Jamal and we haven't said much to each other, but we smile into each other's faces with that connectedness going on. He's really cute and probably only sixteen or seventeen.

And now here I sit with Karissa Bonano and oh. My. Gosh. All these puppy tears run down her face as she apologizes.

"I'm sorry I blew you off at the party. I feel so bad."

"Seth's making you do this."

"No! He's really not. I feel terrible. You know, I know I'm famous and all, and pretty and rich, and pretty much everything any girl wishes she were, and I have been all my life."

You have got to be kidding me.

"I forget that people have feelings sometimes." She adds just the right bit of sorrow to her eyes.

"Because you don't?"

A brow lifts. "No, I don't, Scotty. I guess I really don't. I've always got what I wanted when I wanted it; I never had to really care about anybody."

"But we don't care about people because we want something out of them, Karissa. That's not how it works." I pick up the milk shake. "I've really got to go. I'm sweaty and gross from that costume."

"So, apology accepted?" She puts lip gloss on with her pinky.

I hurry out of the restaurant.

Apology accepted? Give me a break.

She's not *that* good an actress!

There's a part of me that wonders if everything she said was an act. Including the conceited stuff. Does anybody really think that highly of themselves?

Hollywood Nobody: April 19

Hello there, favorite Nobodies! We actually hit the five-hundred-visitors-a-day mark, people, and thanks to you I'm actually starting to feel like a *sort-of somebody*. Sort-of. I'm under no delusion that because I write an anonymous blog that's getting popular that I'm popular. Nobody knows who I am or really where I am! Pretty cool. I love flying under the radar.

But I do feel like we're in this together if you know what I mean.

So.

Today's Rave: Biology! I kid you not. I was reading in

my psych book earlier today that the lovely males of our species unconsciously, innately, look at the lovely females of our species and deep down, some thought at the Y-chromosome levels says, "Yep, she looks healthy enough to bear children."

Most definitely. So if you're starving yourself because you want a boyfriend, guess what, a little meat on those bones is what attracts guys in the first place. Now don't go getting all huge on me, but if you're regular, not looking like one of the <u>Peterby twins</u>, you're fine! More than fine! Now, you naturally skinny girls, you're great too. Nobody's a nobody here at Hollywood Nobody.

Today's Rant: Thong bathing suits. Okay, I just don't want to see big round cheeks. I don't care how toned you are, they look like big *O*s for *overexposed*. All I'm asking for is a relatively decent triangle of fabric back there, doesn't have to be more than five inches or so. Besides, when I see a string rising up out of all that flesh, it just makes me want to start picking at my underwear. You know exactly what I mean, don't you?

Today's Tidbit: Jerry Bryer and Maggie Kane's baby is still yet to be seen. See these pictures after the <u>jump</u>, and you tell me whether or not this baby is for real. Now I've asked some actual women, women with children, whether they think the pregnancy was a fake, and judging by the squareness of her stomach, yes. But judging by the water-weight gain in her arms and legs and face, as well as the skin-blotchiness, they do believe it to be real. But why not show us the child? I mean even the peep of a nose would be nice.

Which, of course, does beg the question: "Do we really need to know?" and aren't they allowed to show their baby to whom they'd like? I'd have to say I guess so. What do you think? Leave your comments.

Hottie Watch: Seth Haas was seen leaving a party scene with Karissa Bonano. Yes, the same Karissa Bonano who had the botched boob job last year. The same Karissa Bonano who has been photographed entering the hotel rooms of at least four rock stars that I can think of off the top of my head. Nothing major between her and Seth as of yet, or so my sources say, but the two were also seen sipping milk shakes at a local diner near the set for the film they're presently working on together. Personally, I think he can do a lot better. How about you?

Today's Quote: "I don't think the money people in Hollywood have ever thought I was normal, but I am dedicated to my work and that's what counts." Angelina Jolie

Later!

Comments:

What is it about you and skinniness? You must weigh a thousand pounds or something.—sickofit, 7:48 a.m.

Seth Hot can totally do better than Karissa Banana. Hate her!—sweet_thing, 8:36 p.m.

Maggie and Jerry do NOT have to show us their baby! For cryin' out loud, they're so popular, they're probably worried about kidnapping or something.—hollywoodjunkie, 9:91 p.m.

Seth rocks!—sethrocks, 8:56 p.m.

Click here to read all the comments.

Tuesday, April 20

Okay, so really, I can't believe I'm reporting like this on Seth and Karissa, but I've got a readership to think of now, a real readership. I'm sure they're all about twelve years old, which is fine. I like people younger than me. They're usually not so idiotic, hormonal, and egocentric.

However, news is news. I worked like crazy on school all day and am finished for the week. Except for math. And now a night shoot is going on at the lighthouse on Ocracoke. Some sort of romantic-dinner-by-the-water scene. So Charley, big loaves of foccacia bread under one arm, a bottle of wine under the other, and a string bag of fruit and cheese (yes, cheese, and I'm completely dying!) hanging from the crook of her elbow, blew out of the house an hour ago.

Darkness settled and I'm thinking I haven't seen my little crabbies in a couple of days, so Jay Gatsby and I head to my spot of beach with a flashlight and a blanket.

I've been developing theories lately about Mr. Bald Biker Dude. Maybe he's obsessed with Charley. But I most definitely have something to do with him, otherwise there'd be no reason for mustard costumes.

And shoot. I don't think I could pry the info from her with ten crowbars. I really don't.

Why does this man want me? Am I the daughter of some famous mobster or something? Oh my gosh! So, what if—now hear me out—years ago Charley got involved with a Michael Corleone type of guy. A young Michael Corleone, not *The Godfather: Part III* Michael Corleone. So Michael falls in love with her. Believe me, I've seen pictures of her when she was young—of course, she was forty when she had me—but she was still a knockout. He falls in love with her somewhere neutral, like at a little restaurant that she runs, some kind of healthy place that serves amazing smoothies and great espresso drinks too. He orders a straight espresso—he's just passing through, you see—sits at the table near the window, and he catches her eye with his bright blue gaze and yes, it's where I get my eyes. From Michael Corleone. From Al Pacino.

I'm absolutely pathetic!

I've got to stop this crazy daydreaming. Besides, I'm Irish.

And let's face it, Al is definitely *not* what he used to be. I mean I met him once and he was pleasant, but the bloom is off the rose if you know what I mean. Thank goodness I can revisit him in his youth whenever I want to on my laptop. I have a secret stash of DVDs underneath my mattress.

Charley would kill me if she knew I had the Godfather DVDs. She's a pacifist. Anything that smacks of violence makes her cry and she's sad enough already.

Seth plops down next to me on the sand. "Hey."

That didn't sound good.

"Hi."

"Karissa told me about your conversation at Ten Clams."

"Wow, you don't mess around, do you? No, 'Hi, Scotty!' or, 'Nice night, huh?'"

He leans back on his hands. "Come on, Scotty, you weren't exactly nice to her."

"I was perfectly cordial."

"You were 'not rude.'"

"So what did I say exactly? You know, you're giving Karissa

the benefit of the doubt here. Don't I deserve a little?"

"I don't know. Let me see if I can parrot the conversation." And he does, pretty much exactly as I remember it.

"So let me get this straight, Seth. She can basically say I'm weird and immature, take you away from your parents for the evening, and you have no problem with that. But I can't excuse myself from her presence without falling all over her and gushing, 'Of course I forgive you, O Perfect Karissa' without you getting upset at me? I think this is all way too junior high."

He sits back up, brushes the sand off his hands. "FYI, Scotty, I gave her real grief over what she did to you, okay?"

"You did?" Wow.

"Uh-huh. That was pretty inexcusable."

"Then why did you disappear for the rest of the night with her?"

"She really is going through some heavy stuff. Really heavy."

I lean forward. "Like what?"

"Can't say."

"Drat." It would have been a great scoop for the blog. I'm horrible, yes, I know.

"You got any coffee?"

"Not tonight. I just wanted to get out of the Y as quick as I could. Hey, Seth?"

"Yeah, Scotty."

"What if she's just yanking your chain? I mean, she could be doing that, you know. You did get onto her, and maybe she just found me to apologize because she wants you."

"I don't know, Scotty . . ."

"I've seen these location romances over and over. You're doing a lot of making out on camera. It's natural, but the question is, do you really want to get involved with Karissa Bonano? She's into drugs and quick relationships and gets drunk a lot—as in, a *lot*. I mean, she could be an alcoholic."

"I don't think she's being anything but straight with me. And you're pretty cynical, Scotty."

"Yeah, well I've been around all this stuff a lot longer than you have."

"And you're a fifteen-year-old girl."

I stand up. That's it. I grab my blanket, book, and flashlight. "So I couldn't possibly know. Is that what you're saying? Good grief, Seth. I haven't taken drugs and slept around, so I couldn't possibly know anything about people, right?" I press the blanket to my chest. "I don't think I'm the one who's naïve here."

And I slip and slide up the dune and over into the space of island where the surf won't pound.

Charley's in the camper when I blow in a few minutes later. "Where were you?!"

"Out on—"

"I've told you to stay close and you're just all over the place these days, Scotty."

"I can't stick around this camper. And we're almost in the middle of nowhere."

"You've seen that guy. He's looking for us."

"Us? Or me? Because you're not the one getting spirited away in a mustard costume all the time."

"You just can't go off by yourself, Scotty!"

I pull off my sweatshirt and throw it into my loft. "I can, Charley. I have to. Do you honestly think I'd survive in this camper by myself all day?" And it hits me, the patheticness of my life, of how I try to sound all cool on my blog, of how I'm so desperate to hang out with Seth Haas and eager to get one up on Karissa Bonano. But each night when I lay down, I feel like a single star in a black night sky.

"I'm lonely, Charley. Can't you understand what it's like to be me?"

She holds out her arms and I sit on the little sofa next to her. I don't cry. I'm not a crier. But I feel her warmth and I love my mother. I really do.

Of course, my thoughts circle back to Seth.

I fear for him. He has no idea what's coming, until *blam*—it's going to hit him square in the face.

A half hour later

Charley goes to bed and so I fire up my laptop and check my e-mail. Grampie wrote!

Hi, Scotty-dear,

Grammie and I made a cheese soufflé for dinner tonight and we thought of you! Wish we could have shared.

We're still at Hatteras. I'm writing an Outer Banks vacation guide for old people. Ha. Ha. Grammie's writing a couple of beach romances. Pretty cute stuff, but then she's a pretty cute old gal.

She just looked over my shoulder and said, "Old? Who's old? Might I remind you that you, sir, are a whole six

months older than I am, and an entire grade higher in
school."
You've got to love Grammie, considering we graduated
from high school almost five decades ago! She also
wrote a poem about how wonderful it is to have a young
friend when you're further along in years. I think she
meant you. Isn't she sweet?
Anyway, I was wondering, as you're still here in the
Outer Banks too, if we might come and take you away
for a few days. If it's okay with your mother, that is. We'll
have a real cheese fest, and I'll grill some steaks if you'd
like.

Are you kidding me? That would be so great! I wonder if
Charley will let me? I bet if I tell her I saw that bald guy skulking
around she'd say yes right away.

Grampie!!!
Let me ask Charley tomorrow. As you might guess, I
have to find the perfect time to do it. Mothers, you know.
Give my love to Grammie! And thanks so much for the
invite. I really, really, really need to get away.
Scotty
P.S. Tell her I can't wait to read the poem!

Two minutes later

I practice until two a.m. all that I'll say to Seth if he ever feels the need to apologize for being, quite frankly, the rudest, most condescending, most gullible person to ever walk the planet.

Wednesday, April 21

This morning, a crisp, bright, and breezy day, it's Joy's for geometry and jewelry. This is great. Most definitely. I'm just racking up the road-school hours. As I unlock my scooter, Seth walks over, hands deep in his pockets. "Scotty."

"Hey, Seth."

"Look, I'm really sorry for what I said."

I grip the handlebars of the scooter. "You have no idea what I've seen or who I am, Seth. You think you do because you're older. But you don't know anything about me. Not really."

I'd actually had a much longer speech prepared, but he just looks so pathetic standing there.

"I know. I'm really sorry."

I sigh. "Well, I forgive you. But I'm still a little miffed."

And he smiles. That Seth Haas crooked grin will earn him multiple millions someday. "How about tomorrow? Will you stop being miffed then?"

I cross my arms.

He peers from beneath his chocolate curls. "I could grill up some bacon?"

I laugh. "Oh, all right. Tomorrow I won't be miffed."

"Cool. Thank you. Gotta go." And he leans forward and gives me a brotherly peck on the cheek. "I really am sorry, Scotty. You're worth more to me than a thousand Karissas."

He runs off on his brown Pumas.

He's only nineteen. I'll be sixteen in five weeks. Would that be creepy? Should I not be feeling the way I feel for him?

Oh man. This is nuts.

This is the first crush I've ever had! I'm so disappointed in myself. I thought I'd get away with skipping this nonsense at least until college. But he's beautiful. Kind. Smart. And nice. Seth Haas is really nice.

Off for theorems and semiprecious stones.

And wouldn't you know it? Jeremy's Jeep is parked at the side of Joy's house.

For one: he's too old for her.

For two: she's too sweet for such a beef jerky guy like Jeremy.

For three: he belongs with Charley.

I clop loudly up the wooden porch steps. Give them fair warning.

"We're around back!" Joy yells.

I inhale down to the arches of my feet.

Jeremy is already on his feet as I open the door to the screen porch. "I'm just going, kiddo. Make some pretty jewelry and stuff."

He winks at me. Joy's eyes are glowing. Really glowing.

She looks so beautiful in a pale yellow sweater, jeans, no makeup except for frosted pink lip gloss.

Crazy, but I can't help being happy for her.

And I don't know what the deal is with Charley and Jeremy, do I? Not at all. For all I know she's been keeping secrets from him all these years too. Jeremy loves me, and that won't change with Joy around. Maybe, like me, Charley's secrets drive him crazy too. But, unlike me, he can choose whether or not to stick around in the fog.

He leans down and kisses Joy on the top of her head.

And when he walks by me he kisses my head too. I look into his eyes. Nothing's changed. Jeremy does love me—I've never doubted that.

"See ya, kid."

"Bye, Jeremy."

A few hours later

I've been all over the Internet trying to make sense of Jesus. A lot of people say he was a really nice guy. Now that counts high in my book, as you know. Some say he was a great teacher. I think they're probably right there and I have so got to get a Bible and at least read the Jesus parts. Because let me tell you, reading this stuff online isn't the same.

Maybe I should see if Grammie and Grampie will get me one. I mean, they don't seem like holy freaks or anything, but they don't seem to be antireligious either.

I type out a quick e-mail to Grampie and send it off.

Back to Google and Jesus.

Oh, man. Way too confusing. Somebody made a fridge

magnet out of Jesus, with little clothes to put on him. Even I know that's just plain wrong.

The little mail harp sounds.

Grampie returned my e-mail already! Grammie, he says, likes reading the Bible sometimes. She said she's got a spare New Testament if that's okay.

Hey, I'll take any testament he's got!

I hurry over to the set. Charley's in the kitchen trailer, hulked over a turkey with a blowtorch. A can of brown spray paint sits on the table beside her.

Stepping up into the trailer I say, "I've been invited to Cape Hatteras to stay with Grammie and Grampie a couple of days, and before you say no, just consider that I may really need a break from all of this."

"Okay."

"Okay, you'll consider? Or okay I can go?"

"You can go."

I shake my head.

"Whoa. Are you serious?"

"Yes." She sets down the blowtorch. "You're really starting to get on my nerves, Scotty."

"What?"

"You've been really depressed and kinda cranky. You know?"

"I have?"

"Yeah. Really, baby."

Okay, so I had no idea. I mean, normally I'm pretty honest with myself about my moods. I guess Seth's getting me down more than I realized. And Jeremy. And The Biker Guy. And shoot, let's just put geometry in there while we're at it.

I run back and e-mail Grampie. I want to know when I can come. "Whenever you'd like," He comes back. "How about the twenty-fifth? Four days from now?"

Perfect.

After unchaining my scooter, I run over to Ten Clams and celebrate with a double grilled-cheese sandwich. Jamal winks at me as he sets it down in front of me.

Hollywood Nobody: April 21

Well, Nobodies, we're up to six hundred unique readers a day and the comments are flying! You all are smart, sassy, and sometimes crazy. I'm lovin' it.

Today's Tidbit: Violette Dillinger's album is number four on Billboard. She doesn't have a creepy manager father. Her mom's a nurse. She's from rural Virginia. She doesn't grunt out her songs and you actually hear the melody she's singing. Maybe there's hope. She's playing tonight here in Boston. Check in and let us know how it was if you get to the concert.

Today's Quote: "They're not going to be turning me into any freak show!" Violette Dillinger

Today's Rant: Chloë Sevigney's wardrobe. Everybody's always raving about this young actress's dresses. Does anybody else find it just plain weird? I don't get it. Is this just a modern retelling of *The Emperor's New Clothes*?

Today's Rave: Gwyneth Paltrow. Check out this picture. She is looking good! Healthy and like a fresh, young mom who's

actually borne children. The pathetic factor? Not found here!
Later!

Comments:
Caught Violette's show! It was awesome. The girl actually has talent, unlike some other (cough, cough) young female entertainers these days. –pickin_violets, 3:46 a.m.

Hollywood Nobody! You are the best! Fans of your blog made a strong showing at the concert last night! Consider your blog Word One for me! I'll keep you posted and send everyone your way. —Violette, 10:34 a.m.

A second later

I'm not going to write about Seth today. I'm still a little miffed.

Thursday, April 22

After checking my blog comments I want to scream! Yes. Exclusive, first-news privilege for Violette Dillinger! I e-mail her and we IM for an hour. Her agent says it's cool, grass roots and stuff. And she's really nice too.

The bummer? I can't tell a soul! Especially Seth. I already have the first-news rights on him whether he knows it or not. Not that I'll see him. I've got plans for today.

Field trip!

Naturally, I've been all over the Internet researching Ocracoke Island, getting all my ducks in a row, as they say, for my history unit.

This place overflows with history, swarms with sea captains, life-saving stations, fishermen, and even piracy. You've got to love a place that actually has a pirate or two tucked in its footlocker.

In this case, it's Blackbeard, aka Edward Teach, born in England back in the sixteen hundreds. According to an engraving, he had a dreadlocked beard. Pretty crazy stuff.

A fog rolled in today and I'm headed over to Ocracoke to see Teach's Hole, where Blackbeard made his last stand, where his ghost supposedly still wanders, looking for its decapitated head.

Spooky.

I'm walking today. I need the exercise after that double cheese sandwich yesterday. I swear, I went back home, did a little geometry and was asleep by eight. Not that it mattered. Seth has been hanging out with Karissa nonstop. He keeps going on with "we're just friends" and "I'm not a fool, Scotty, I know she's not exactly a nice girl" as if I buy any of it and was I really stupid to have a crush on an older guy like that in the first place.

I should have known better.

But it felt good to feel like that. I'm not gonna lie.

Do you ever wander down the road and forget to look around you, only to find yourself at your destination, wondering how you got there?

I'm standing on the shore by Teach's Hole, looking out over

the sound. The mists and the fog dance in swirling steps and the seagulls cry. So really, is there a treasure buried somewhere down there, obscured one day when a raging storm pushed its waters into new places?

Well, most people say Blackbeard was quite the big spender, and the possibility of him leaving a treasure around here is slim. Like Lara Flynn Boyle slim? Or Kate Winslet slim? That could make all the difference in the world.

Now, Blackbeard could have given any Hollywood celebrity a run for his or her money. First of all, the man was lousy at marriage, as his fourteen wives might confirm. Fourteen! I should send an e-mail to Liz Taylor and comfort her with that fact. Maybe I will. Liz has contacted me on my birthday, one way or another, usually through Jeremy, since I was eight.

So I sit on the shore, gather my feet up beneath me, pull a legal pad out of my backpack and begin to write, gazing out over the misty waters from time to time, seeing a phantom boat, ragged men pulling at the oars, a man with a snaky beard shouting for them to move faster, ye scurvy curs! A fog kisses their shaved heads; they laugh through rotted teeth.

Maybe I could hail them from my perch and sail the high seas, away from the Y, Charley, Seth, and this sad life of isolation where it takes the popularity of an anonymous blog to make me feel like somebody.

I'm excited about visiting two senior citizens at an RV park, for heaven's sake!

I'm just sayin'.

Right. Three pages on Blackbeard finished. I'll type it up at home and stick it in my file.

Maybe my dad was a pirate.

Played by Al Pacino.

Next stop: Styron's Boat Rentals for a trip to Portsmouth Island. A deserted village still resides upon the flat expanse of land along with some houses, a church, and the old lifesaving station, all in good repair due to the local "Friends of Portsmouth." Yes, I've already been all over the Internet on this one too.

But first, lunch at Ten Clams.

Oh, wouldn't you know it! Seth sits in *our* booth with Karissa. She wears a luscious brown mohair sweater and a pair of chocolate leather pants. High-heeled boots, hair in a sleek bun at the back of her head. Plain gold hoops.

They're holding hands across the table.

And I dressed for comfort in jeans and a GAP sweatshirt. A *GAP* sweatshirt. My hair is in its usual ponytail and I forgot to put earrings in. Makeup? Yeah right. Who's going to wear makeup when you're researching Blackbeard the pirate? I mean, he's dead; he couldn't care less, right? Turning toward the door, I *will* make my escape. He's too involved in Karissa's powder-blue eyes to see me. I push on the doorknob.

"Scotty! Hey!"

Shoot.

I turn and smile. Give a little wave.

"Why are you leaving?" He stands up.

"I forgot something back at the RV."

"Well come have a quick cup of coffee or something."

"Nah, that's okay."

Karissa looks around. Oh, no makeup! Her face is bare. "Scotty, come on over. We were just talking about you."

Great.

There's absolutely no way to get out of this gracefully. Five minutes. That's all I'll stay; and then I'm gone, over to Portsmouth Island for some highly preferable deserted buildings and wind-swept grasses.

"Hi, guys!" I wave a little. Again. How lame.

"Scoot in." Seth steps aside. Darn. No easy exit from the inside seat of the booth. I swear he's doing that on purpose.

I slide over toward the window, sitting as far against the wall as I can. "How are you?" I ask Karissa.

"Good. Glad it's cloudy. We had to suspend the shoot for today."

"No interior shots left?" I ask.

"No." She fiddles with an amber pendant. "Just a few more sunny beach shots and then we'll wrap."

"Quick shoot. But that's Jeremy." I reach back and divide my ponytail in two, pulling the sections toward my scalp and tightening the band. "I'll be here longer, of course."

"Why is that?" Seth asks.

"Jeremy, Charley, and I usually vacation for a few days together afterward. Enjoy the local color, the scenery, the food. Jeremy always lets me eat whatever I want, and Charley doesn't seem to mind."

Karissa. "So you and Jeremy are tight?"

"She's like his daughter." Seth.

"So you really have been around this business all of your life?"

"Yeah. Most definitely."

"Wow." She rests her chin on her hand. "You seem so normal. No offense! Really!"

"I thought I was weird."

"No. You're weird because you're normal. If that makes sense."

I sit up a little. I think that's the nicest thing anybody's said to me in a long time.

An hour or so later

In my mind I'm hearing that mournful Clint Eastwood movie song "They Call the Wind Moriah," as I venture around the island of Portsmouth by myself. If this were the Old West, I'd expect to see a tumbleweed roll on by, a hawk circling overhead, hear saloon doors swish on their creaky hinges. I do have a whistling wind sweeping off the Pamlico Sound, however.

Or, getting back to pirates, it's even easier to see masts and sails materializing on the ocean's horizon, and here I stand, all alone, guarding the big black X, a rapier at my side, tall boots covering my legs from mid-thigh southward, voluminous sleeves flapping in the wind like spinnakers.

It's a self-guided tour. Fred—the weathered man with the skin of an avocado, only peach colored, who brought me over in his boat—wasn't feeling well. "A bit unsettled in the stomach." He stayed by his boat, lying back with his cap over his eyes and halfway to sleeping before I'd walked ten yards. Fine with me. I'd rather haunt the place myself.

First stop, the post office. Now this is interesting. The glass cases and the wall shelves, none of them holding much, have obviously been cared for, polished, shined, dusted. The last mail that went out of here was in the thirties I believe. This whole island was deserted in 1972, after Henry Piggott died. I'll tour his house too.

Man! Talk about a life exactly the opposite of mine. I swear, I could just move in here. Take my own little boat over to Ocracoke for supplies and books and a chat with folks who'd come to know me as "that nice girl from out on Portsmouth." I'd love that. Charley could travel around on her own and leave me home on the island, waiting for her to come back. I'd use an outhouse for those necessities, and kerosene would heat my little wood-and-window home, complete with a foundation and a roof, and I'd cook my food at a gas range. Canned goods mostly.

If a hurricane blew in, well, I'd certainly be smart enough to get out when the first warnings came over the battery-powered wireless radio on the shelf above the fireplace. I'd meet up with Joy and we'd travel onto the mainland together.

Dream on.

I head over to the church, a tidy green and white building, steeple directing all eyes toward the heavens. The mists have cleared, but the sky remains shot through with iron, pewter, and silver, and it smells like rain. I'd better hurry.

I turn to look at the ocean.

The bushes around the side of the church rustle.

A big rustle.

Not a wind rustle.

What?

The hair on the back of my neck stands up and I step forward. Now, in the movies, when somebody hears something and starts going toward the dangerous noise, I always yell, "Just run, you idiot!" not realizing then, as I do now, that curiosity really does get the better of you. So I tiptoe around the corner.

And there he stands.

Biker Guy!

He steps forward and I grab the handles on my backpack and run. I don't have to be frozen in my tracks like the female characters in movies. I haul! And I promise myself I will *not* fall like they invariably do.

"Wait!" he yells.

Yeah right! Like I'm going to wait for him. He wants to kill me. Or Charley. Or something.

And he's definitely *not* Al Pacino.

Luckily he's heavy. Heavier than I earlier realized.

"Ariana!" he yells. "Please!"

His feet pound on the turf, but I'm fifteen and he's, what, fifty? There's no way.

"Start the boat!" I scream to Fred, who sits up with a jerk. "Help!"

"Ariana! Wait!"

Ariana?

Who's Ariana?

Biker Guy is gaining on me. Dear God, don't let him pull out a gun or anything.

Fred, eyes as round as baseballs, pulls the cord on the outboard motor and unties it from the dock. He holds onto the planking with one hand.

My muscles start to scream but I push forward and finally, grabbing Fred's hand, I sail off my feet and land in the boat. He shoves off and feeds the motor more gas.

"Wait, Ariana! Wait please!" The man stands at the end of the dock, hands on his knees as he struggles for breath. He reaches into his pocket and I scream.

But he only wipes his forehead with a red bandana.

I stare at him as he gets smaller and smaller and, finally, is covered by fog that rolls in across the steely waters.

Forty-five minutes later

I don't care what they're doing and I don't care who sees. I run into Jeremy's trailer, where he's head to head with Seth and Karissa. "Where's Charley? She wasn't at the trailer."

"In town at the IGA. We've got a shoot this afternoon at the diner. I realized we could . . . never mind. This isn't a good time, kid. I've got other things to plan for with this change of weather."

"That Biker Guy almost got to me." I'm practically shouting. "So if you don't mind, Mr. Director, timing isn't very crucial to me at the moment."

Seth stands up and lays a hand on my shoulder. "Are you okay, Scotty?"

I shrug it off. "Not hardly."

Karissa stands beside Seth.

"Look, Jeremy, I've got to get off this island. Right now. The ferry is leaving in ten minutes. I've got a place to go, but I've got to speak to Charley."

Won't Grammie and Grampie be surprised to find me on their stoop three days early?

Jeremy motions to the assistant director. "Take over." He slides off his chair and takes my hand. "Let's go. I'll get you to the ferry. We'll pick up Charley on the way."

We practically run to his truck.

"Scotty!" Seth yells.

But I ignore him. I just can't right now. He's got Karissa and a film career and a great family, and I've got a lying mother and a big bald man trying to get me in what could be a case of mistaken identity, if his calling me Ariana means anything. Clearly, I've got other things to think about.

Jeremy opens my door and jumps into the driver's seat. As we whiz over to the IGA, he calls Charley. "Be waiting outside. He almost got her this time. We're taking her to the ferry." And then he makes another call to one of the grips, Willis. "Code blue. Hide the Y." Pause. "Take it onto Ocracoke and put it behind Joy's house." And he rattles off the address like he owns the place or something.

When he skids to a stop in front of the supermarket, I move over to the middle of the bench seat and Charley climbs in.

"What happened, Scotty?"

I tell her everything. It happened so fast, I realize, that there's little to tell. But I zero in on the one new fact. "Who's Ariana, Charley? He kept yelling for Ariana. This may all be a case of mistaken identity. I mean, he may be looking for somebody else!"

Jeremy grips the wheel. "It's no case of mistaken identity, kid. She can't tell you who Ariana is."

"Why? Will she have to kill me?" I mean, maybe my mafia scenario is true!

"No. But you'll be in greater danger."

"How can I be in greater danger than I am now?"

Charley grabs my knee. "Are you sure you can get Grammie and Grampie to come down to meet you at the ferry?"

"Yes. I'll call right now."

So I do because, obviously, the subject of Ariana is closed. Because they say so. This is absolutely ridiculous. I am so furious!

But hearing Grammie's voice and her reassuring, "Of course, dear!" soothes me. But then it makes me mad all over again, because Charley should be doing that, not some RV lady!

When we get to the ferry, Jeremy hands me five twenties. "Here, kiddo. Stay there until we wrap. The Cape Hatteras KOA, right?"

I nod.

Before I walk into the boat, Charley hugs me. "I'm sorry, baby. I'm really sorry."

"Yeah, right, Charley."

I hide myself in the ladies' room for the entire trip across the dark waters. Like I said, I'm not a crier. But right now, I sure wish I was.

Dear Elaine,

I'm sitting in the bathroom stall on a ferryboat. The Biker Guy could be outside somewhere for all I know, walking in-between the cars and peering into the windows. I doubt it, really. First of all, I have no idea how he got onto Portsmouth Island in the first place, but I doubt it was easy. Probably a rowboat or something.

I don't trust anyone anymore. While I was lonely and sad, I thought that was the worst. But now I know better. There's nobody I can really rely on anymore. I'll be honest, I thought maybe Seth was that guy. Not that he'd whisk me away romantically, right? Or maybe I hoped he would, somehow. I don't know. I'm foolish I guess.

Jeremy's obviously tight with Charley on all of this. I can't trust him. And I certainly can't trust Charley, not if she won't even tell me who Ariana is.

Ariana. It's a beautiful name. Very oceanic. Like a name a mermaid would be given by her gorgeous mother before the two are tragically separated by the evil sea-squid king.

Okay, so I just looked up the name on babynames.com and it's Italian, meaning Very Holy. So it's definitely not me.

New subject. I can't think about this anymore right now. It's scaring me.

So here's what I've been thinking lately: I think that whole church service was bunk. A big show. Some people would say, "Well, maybe they're sincere," but I don't think so. I've been around show business all my life and I smell it when I see it. A show is a show is a show. I just can't imagine Jesus saying those things, even though I don't know much about him. He wouldn't be mad at me for going to hell, would he? I think he'd be very, very sad.

Is that all faith is about anyway, escaping something bad? I know what *that* feels like. I'm living it with Charley. We escape all the time and never grow closer together.

So where's Al Pacino when you need him? Maybe he'd have some answers. And what about my dad? Does he even know I exist? That's my question of the day, because as secretive as Charley is about this Ariana girl, I'm sure she was as equally secretive about me where Dad is concerned. I'll bet she never even gave him the chance to love me.

Oh my gosh! What if Biker Guy *is* my dad?!

No. No way. I don't even want to consider that. I'm having a hard enough time with Charley right now as it is.

So here I sit, shaking in a bathroom stall on a boat. Did he think of this when he had sex with my mother—that one day, because of his act, his offspring would be sitting all by herself in a bathroom stall on a boat, escaping a man who may want her dead?

This is why you don't just go screwing around all the time, Dad. I hope to goodness you're a little bit more responsible these days. Then again, if you didn't screw around, I wouldn't be here. Come on! Can't anything be straightforward and easy?

I just can't handle these thoughts right now.

Forty minutes later

Grammie and Grampie wait on the dock, holding hands and waving. She's wearing white. He's wearing navy blue. I throw myself into their arms and cry, and cry, and cry.

Friday, April 23

I awaken, safe in Grammie and Grampie's Beaver Marquis and the smell of bacon frying is even better than the coffee brewing. Knowing Grampie, it's gourmet bacon and gourmet coffee.

Grammie sits down on the pull-out sofa, and of course, they unearthed a comforter softer than Grampie's reassurances last night when I burst into tears and told them everything.

Grammie cooed and Grampie said, "There, there," over and over again as they held me.

"Morning, sunshine." She pats my hand. "Get a good sleep?"

"Really good."

She smiles, reaching out her other hand to brush an errant tendril of hair from my eyes.

"Grampie making bacon?"

"And sausage."

I look over at Grampie, who gives me a thumbs-up. "You know we'll take care of you, Scotty."

Really, Grampie? Will you really? Man, I wish they really were my grandparents.

Grammie stands to her feet. "Now, grapefruit juice or orange?"

"A Coke?" I throw her a sheepish grin.

"A Coke! Of course!"

"I'll get it." Grampie opens the full-sized refrigerator. "With ice, right?"

"If you don't mind."

I throw back the covers and by the time I'm out of the bathroom, the bed's been returned to its sofa status, the linens put away. A tall, sweating glass of Coke sits on the dinette.

Grammie invites me to sit down across from her. "Now, Scotty, we've got plans like you wouldn't believe. First off, we'll head up to the Currituck lighthouse and, well, that will be a gorgeous drive. We're going to rent motorcycles because it's a gorgeous day. Grampie's getting a sidecar for you!"

Oh, my gosh. Could they get any better, these two?

"And then, we'll head over to a German restaurant and eat sausages and Wiener schnitzel and spaetzle covered with copious amounts of butter, from a cow I might add!"

"I'm so there."

"I knew you would be." Grammie tucks a tuft of white hair into her bright pink turban.

Grampie sets down three plates. Bacon, sausage patties, scrambled eggs with cheese, and homemade white-flour-and-lard biscuits. Not one thing on the entire plate I'm allowed to eat. I tell him this as he sits down next to Grammie.

He winks and we fall into our breakfast like none of us has eaten in days.

Hollywood Nobody: April 23

Good morning, Nobodies! I've got a big day ahead of me, so let's just cut to the chase.

Today's Rant: Hair extensions. Fear not, little ones. When you see a head of hair on one of Hollywood's finest that resembles that of a <u>Barbie Doll</u>, chances are it's not entirely, completely, or even remotely her hair. So you can use all the body-building shampoo you want, tease your hair so it looks like you belong in an eighties girl band, or heck, drive around all day in a convertible, and it's just not going to look like that. Please, do yourself a favor and realize: Most Of This Stuff Is Fake! Just to show you what I mean, look at these pictures of stars in their natural state after the jump. I swear, if Pamela Anderson or Christina Aguilera walked by you on the street in their natural state, you wouldn't take any more notice of them than they might you.

The scary thing? I actually think, judging by how they act when I meet them from time to time, some of these people really believe they *are* that gorgeous, even though they've been pulled and clipped and stuffed and squeezed and extended. Makes me love Jaime Lee Curtis more and more. Although, I did hear a rumor she had plastic surgery lately. True or not? Stay tuned.

Today's Quote: (It's the best!) "Ah, stardom! They put your name on a star in the sidewalk on Hollywood Boulevard and you walk down and find a pile of dog manure on it. That tells the whole story, baby." Lee Marvin

Today's Rave: Reese Witherspoon. Again. Love her! Once again she's on the beach with her kids, being a mom. I applaud every ounce of success the woman achieves.

Today's News: Seth Hottie Haas wraps up his shoot soon. He and Karissa Bonano were seen holding hands on the beach. See the picture after the jump. You decide. Hot and heavy? Or just friends?

Violette Dillinger Stats:

Age: 17

Hometown: Baltimore

Hair: dark brown

Religion: Baptist (I kid you not!)

Favorite Musical Artist: Billy Joel

Favorite Artist Artist: Lee Krasner

Favorite Food: her mom's homemade cinnamon rolls

Orientation: straight

Long Term Goals: Get that last English class finished, save up lots of money, go to Yale and become a doctor.

Least Favorite Thing: straightening irons

I knew I loved that gal!

Later!

Comments:

Too many to list these days, but hollywoodjunkie is still usually the first to comment. What? Does she hang around online waiting for me to post? I'm just sayin! –hnobody, 9:26 a.m.

A minute later

I feel like such a squidge posting a picture from my cell phone, but shoot, maybe I'm helping Seth get used to what it feels like when your life is no longer your own. Man, I hope he doesn't find out about this blog! I'm up to seven hundred readers a day. And I'm still anonymous.

See, I have to admit I do read the celebrity gossip blogs, and some of these guys are just prima donnas, biting people with their acid mouths and then, when they get the first nod from the celebrity they've chewed to shreds, suddenly they're all buddy-buddy. It's gross.

Well not me.

"Scotty?"

I look up from my screen and practically jump out of my skin.

Grampie laughs. "You ready to go? I've got the Tracker loaded up, and we'll head over to the rental place to pick up the bikes."

"And then, the wind on our faces, eating up the miles we'll go?"

"That's right, honey."

Grammie ties a zebra-print scarf around her white hair. "I love riding bikes. Reminds me of the old days, doesn't it, George?"

"Oh yeah, Billie Jo."

"You guys were bikers?"

Grampie reaches for Grammie's hand. "Once upon a time."

Man, you just never know with people, do you?

An hour and twenty minutes later

The sidecar feels dangerous, thrilling, invigorating, like if you took a mentholated cough drop and made it an experience. I watch the solid white line beside me, the tufts of grass, the trees, and arch my gaze into the wide blue sky. Did I say these people know how to live?

Cheese, cheese, and more cheese. For lunch we pull into a little beachy bistro in the village of Duck, deciding to save the German restaurant for dinner. So, the menu if you please, at least for me, includes:

Appetizer: Mozzarella Sticks

Soup: Mexican Cheese Soup

Meal: Triple Fromage Grilled-Cheese Sandwich

Dessert: Yep, Cheesecake.

Heaven has descended. A stringy, melty, yummy heaven. Grammie and Grampie, eating spinach salads, watch me shovel in the dairy products, smiles sweetening their faces. I swear, at one time, Grampie actually teared up, his blue eyes melting, and Grammie saw and misted over as well.

They must be pretty lonely, really, for the sight of a strange girl eating cheese to render them emotional.

And hey, if it means so much to them, I am happy to oblige, shoveling it in with even more gusto.

Forty-five minutes later

We stand by the hill on which the Wright brothers made that famous flight.

"Grampie and Grammie? Did you ever feel you wanted to fly? Like you know you were made to, but you hadn't yet found your wings? That they were somewhere on your body, but you just couldn't seem to locate them?"

Grampie puts his arm around my shoulders. "I felt that way for most of my youth, honey."

"Me too," says Grammie. "It's harder for some of us to find our way."

"I have no idea what I want to do with my life."

"You're only fifteen, dear." Grammie.

"Almost sixteen."

"Yes. On June the sixth." Grampie.

I turn to him. "How do you know that?"

He looks startled. "Well. I . . . I . . . you must have told me at one time."

Grammie. "George isn't usually so good with dates. Count yourself as in high standing with the man."

"That's right!" Grampie practically shouts.

"Well, I just wish I'd get some sort of vision. I love reading. I love computers. I love history. But I can't picture giving my life completely to any of them."

The downer here? I should be able to have these talks with Charley. But hey, Grammie and Grampie don't mind a bit, and that's saying something. Like maybe they were sent my way.

Grampie leads us to a bench and we sit down. "Listen, Scotty, and hear me well because I'm not prone to give advice, and rarely do I say it twice."

"That's true." Grammie nods and settles next to me. She extends an open tin of mints and I take one. So does Grampie.

"You have time. Do you hear me? There's so much pressure these days to decide things before you even know what's out there."

He's right.

"Scotty, you have the opportunity before you that not many young women your age do. You're traveling around, seeing things, meeting new people all the time. And you can learn from these things. I mean, look where we are." He sweeps his hand over the dunes. "How many children learn about the Wright brothers but never see where they made that first flight, a flight that we both know changed the world as we know it?"

He's right.

"I know you're lonely. And I'm sorry. I don't have an answer for that. But I guess the best any of us can do is make the most of what we're given. Concentrate on the good things, not the things which are lacking."

He's right yet again.

Grammie takes my hand. "And we're always here for you, Scotty. You must know that, or at least, if you don't, hear it now."

"Really?" I ask.

"Yes." Grampie. "You just call and we'll come running."

"But I live such a crazy life on such a crazy schedule, in such *secrecy!*"

"We'll never be far away." Grampie.

"Why would you care so much?"

The two shrug. "Sometimes you just can't help yourself." Grammie.

On the way back from the German restaurant, where I stuffed myself with meat, meat, meat, we pass a little church, white and simple. Looking as if it has withstood the elements for many years, it reminds me of the chapel on Portsmouth Island. On the sign a simple message in black letters stands out against the glowing background.

Jesus cares.

I look up at Grampie, face to the wind, hands gripped on the handlebars of the bike as he guides us back home.

Is that what that sign means? Jesus really cares about me? That maybe he was the one who sent Grammie and Grampie my way?

So now, as I lie on the pull-out sofa, wrapped in my fluffy comforter, I think about the day, and I think maybe I was looking for Jesus in all the wrong places: tent meetings, websites, dead preachers. Who knew I'd run into him in a Beaver Marquis at a run-of-the-mill KOA?

Saturday, April 24

Grammie and Grampie are tucked into their bedroom and I can't sleep. Twelve thirty a.m. So I pull out my laptop and open her up.

There seems to be a lot of Christian RVer stuff online and around the campgrounds, so I figure . . . why not? After an easy enough Google, I find myself in a chatroom. People are signed in from all over the country.

Admittedly, I just love RVers. I really do. There's something inherently adventurous about people who will sell their house, sock the money into a tin can on wheels, and hit the road for the rest of their lives. I don't think they imagine they'll ever be really sick or disabled, because if you're planning for that, you'd *never* put your life on the road.

So by default, they're optimistic too.

And since teenagers are such a rare commodity during the school year, well, I guess it isn't any wonder I'm one of the darlings. It shouldn't surprise me that Grammie and Grampie have become devoted. It really shouldn't.

So here I sit watching an interplay between FiddleGirl and CrossTones.

They're musicians who travel around the country! Kind of a life like ours, actually. He's a gospel singer and she's a fiddle player who performs at Scottish and Irish festivals all over. Maybe there's a budding romance.

I hop on in, telling them I'm a teenager on the road, and they're so curious and kind. FiddleGirl IMs me privately.

FiddleGirl: It must be kinda lonely for you.

LoveChild: Yeah. But I'm trying to learn to see the good.

FiddleGirl: The Bible says to do that. Good for you.

LoveChild: I'm not a Christian, though. I'm trying to figure things out. Which is why I came to this room. I've met nice people on the RV circuit. Christian people. So, I don't know where I am.

FiddleGirl: That's okay. God does.

LoveChild: You really think so?

FiddleGirl: With all my heart.

I find out her name's Maisie and she's really nice. And you know how important "nice" is to me. She says to put her on my "friends" list, so I do. She puts me on hers.

About five hours later

The clock on the microwave reads 5:45 a.m.

I flip open my vibrating cell phone. "Hey, Charley."

"Hi, baby. Sorry it's early. I'm about to head to the set. You doin' okay?"

"Yeah. Grammie and Grampie are great."

"Jeremy and I think you should be fine to return in a couple of days."

"No sign of Biker Guy?"

"Nobody matching his description on the island that any of us can see. And I haven't received any phone calls alerting me."

"Who makes those calls anyway?"

"I'll save that for later, but suffice it to say they're always right. Although they slipped up twice on this shoot. Those surprise times."

"How much does Jeremy know about the situation, Charley?"

"Pretty much everything."

"Is Jeremy my father?"

"Definitely not."

"You said that awfully fast."

"Baby, I'm really, honest-to-goodness telling you the truth. Jeremy isn't your father."

"How do I know that for sure?"

She sighs. "You can't. I think I've made a real mess of things."

"So when will you tell me the truth?"

"When the truth won't possibly hurt you."

"So for now, I'm in danger. You're hiding *me*, Ariana or whatever my real name is, from somebody because they want me for some crazy reason only you and Jeremy know."

"That pretty much sums it up."

"So I *am* Ariana?"

"Yes."

"I need to know more. Come on, Charley. I already know things aren't what they seem. You might as well tell me everything."

"Not on the phone."

"When we get back then."

"I'll make us a special dinner."

Uh . . . no thanks. I can't imagine what it'll be.

"That'll be great."

And now I feel sick. My stomach feels like an anthill, because sometimes the truth is something you wish you hadn't asked for.

Almost three hours later

Saturday is the perfect beach day, I have to say. Even for a person like me, who's basically not chained to a schedule of any kind, Saturday always holds a bit of mystery, a realm without boundaries, and the sun should always shine. Even if it doesn't, though, there's something about the pitter-patter of Saturday raindrops that sounds better than those hitting Monday through Friday. Sunday raindrops I hate even worse.

So when Grammie suggests we pack a picnic and haul some chairs down to the beach, Grampie starts making sandwiches he calls Dagwoods. "From that Blondie comic on the funny pages," he explains as he fries up some bacon strips.

"I know of it." I slice some Havarti cheese. "Just never heard the sandwiches called that in real life."

He winks and snaps the tongs at me like the jaws of an alligator. "Stick with me, honey."

Grammie breezes in with a sun hat in each hand. "Now, Scotty, you have a delicate complexion like I do, and don't let the time of year fool you! Spring sunshine can still do a number on your skin. Which hat would you prefer?"

One is a wide-brimmed hat, natural straw, with a brown gros-grain ribbon. Very gardener-chic. The other is baby-blue with a huge white rose. Very costume design. Classy costume design, however, like something Edith Head or one of her minions would create. "I'll take that one." I point to the gardener-chic.

She places it on the sofa. "I knew you'd say that!"

About thirty minutes later we've constructed three triple-decker sandwiches with bacon, Havarti, smoked turkey, avocado, tomato and chipotle sauce. "Mild," Grampie says. "For Billie Jo's sake."

"Fine by me!" I scoop up my backpack thinking I'll finish up *The Great Gatsby* today, and I can't believe Daisy. She has the worst ability to handle men that I've ever seen. Or maybe the best. Sometimes it's just hard to tell. Some women gravitate toward the jerks, don't they?

I think maybe Charley was like that once upon a time. But she doesn't date anymore, so I can't really know.

Forty minutes later

And now, feet in the sand, hat on my brow, Grammie writing one of her dime-store novels on a notepad and Grampie reading through the latest edition of *Newsweek*, the sun shines on our pale shins and calves. It's cool, the breeze nippy, but Grammie remembered some fleece blankets to wrap around our shoulders.

After an hour or so I set down *Gatsby*. "There. Finished. Again."

"How many times have you read that, dear?" Grammie lays her pen on her pad.

"Three now."

She shuffles her feet. "I always loved that book." Grampie's walking along the shore, "keeping fit," as he says. Grammie laughs. "But then I've always loved parties."

"I hate them."

Horror elongates her face. "No! That can't be!"

"It really is."

"Well, we're about to change all that."

Oh no.

She imitates the look on my face perfectly and wags a finger at me. "Now, now. Tomorrow night is a dance at the RV park and you're going."

"I'll be the youngest person there."

"And the most beautiful."

Oh, Grammie. She needs an eye exam.

After lunch

Grammie and I step into a colorful quaint boutique up in Kitty Hawk. I imagine this area is hopping come mid-June, but for now just the two of us wander the store on a street almost deserted. I love almost deserted.

Actually, I kinda like deserted too.

It's when a bunch of people come together, milling about like insects or rodents, that's when I get antsy. And speaking of the dance, I can't believe I let her talk me into it.

On second thought, I can.

There isn't much I wouldn't do for Grammie. She gave me her poem last night called "Young Old Friends." I'm going to memorize it.

I let her pick out the dress, as she's paying for it and only people sixty-five-years-old and up will be there so I might as well look pretty for them.

And she cries when I come out of the dressing room. "I feel like I'm helping you pick out your prom dress!"

I smile and think, "I wouldn't be caught dead in this aqua dress," but instead I hug her and her warmth. Her flowery smell and her cherry breath on my cheek take my heart away to a place called love.

"You make me feel like a princess, Grammie."

That is completely true and has nothing to do with the dress.

Sunday, April 25

Well, I sure am the hit tonight!

I have to admit, the dress wasn't all that bad once we purchased coordinating jewelry and high-heeled silver shoes with a T-strap. I look a little Gatsby maybe?

Grampie says, "Absolutely, honey!"

Thank goodness I've had to learn to dance in my bit parts on films. And the old men are kind. They don't try to do anything fancy, and maybe they're too old to anyway, but my dance card is full.

Yes, there are dance cards here.

I whirl around the floor in slow waltzes, a fox trot and even shag to some beach music. I dance with Ed and Sal, Jim, Frank, and Roger. I even dance with a Humbert.

Of course, Grampie fills in some slots, and I save him the last dance.

The band begins "String of Pearls." Grampie takes my hand and swings me onto the floor. "Having a good time, honey?"

"This is great. I don't know why I thought it would be a drag."

He laughs. "We'll all sleep good tonight! Especially you! You are the belle of the ball."

Yeah, I guess I am.

Humbert waves.

The door to the activity room opens and a dark-haired young man walks in and looks around the room. It's Seth.

Seth!

Seth Haas, right here at the RV park, and even I'd be a fool not to admit I'm the reason he came.

I finish the dance with Grampie. I know who my main man is these days. But wow, Seth looks as handsome as I've ever seen him in nice jeans, loafers, and a gold windbreaker. He waves as I swirl by and I lift some of my fingers from Grampie's shoulder and wiggle them.

Grampie notices.

"Is that young man here for you, honey?"

"Yes, Grampie. He's from the film shoot."

"Come to take you back to Toledo, I guess."

"I suppose."

He sighs. "I thought we'd get to keep you until at least tomorrow." The music ends; he takes hold of my shoulders and holds me at arm's length, smiling. "You watch that guy."

I laugh. "He's just a friend, Grampie, really. Really, really." I lean forward. "He's nineteen."

"Too old for you and don't you forget it."

"I absolutely won't."

Grampie leads me over to Seth. He holds out his hand. "I'm George Wethington."

"Seth Haas." Seth shakes his hand. "Pleasure to meet you, sir."

Grampie shrugs. "Well, at least he's got manners."

I squeeze Grampie's arm. "He is an actor, don't forget."

"Oh, my. Why did you have to tell me that?"

"Are you here to take me back to the shoot?"

Seth nods. "Charley was going to come with Jeremy and I asked them if it was okay if I did it. They resisted, but I can be pretty persuasive."

"Crazy stuff." Grampie. "Did things seem back to normal down there?"

"Yes, sir. As far as most people could see, Charley and Scotty were gone, as in left completely. But that's all I know about anything."

"Okay then." Grampie points toward the door. "Follow me back to the RV and we'll get her packed up and ready to go."

Grammie runs over. "Don't tell me Scotty's leaving?"

"Afraid so, Billie Jo."

"With *him*?"

We all laugh.

"See, Seth?" I say. "Not everybody's enamored of film actors."

Seth raises his brows. "Obviously not. I think I'm in love." He bows to Grammie.

Grammie blushes and Grampie rolls his eyes. "Don't take it personally, young man. My wife is a hopeless romantic." He puts his arm around her. "And I aim to make sure she stays that way." He plants a tender kiss upon her temple, and she blushes more deeply.

Seventy-five minutes later

Seth drives in a manly way, like he grew up driving trucks on a farm or something. His beautiful hands handle the steering wheel of Jeremy's old truck with ease as we speed down the road to the last ferry.

"We're cutting it close, but I think we'll just make it," he says.

"Hopefully you won't have to resort to crashing through the barricade, sailing through the air and onto the deck of the boat."

"I'm an actor, not a stunt driver."

"Let's just hope you stay sane enough to let the professionals do your stunts for you."

"Definitely. I'm not going to do my own stunts. Ever." He grins. "I mean, I wouldn't want to put a stuntman out of a job or anything."

"Certainly not."

We smile into each other's eyes.

Windows down, the truck plows through the nippy, salty sea air. I love the smell, the humidity of life by the shore. The heater, blowing full blast, warms our feet and faces. "I think, if I could ever settle down and live in one place, it would be near the beach," I say.

"East Coast or West?"

"Oh, gosh. East. I love the thought that France is on the other side for some reason."

"Must be the cheese over there."

"Maybe that's it."

He knows me. That's kinda cool.

I grip the armrest on the door. "So, where's Karissa?"

"She left for LA early this morning."

Which explains why he's here instead. Drat.

"She wasn't supposed to leave until tomorrow."

Seth pulls up to the tollbooth, pays the fee, and allows one of the workers to direct him onto the ferry. Not many people are traveling over to Ocracoke so late. Oh, that's right. It's only nine o'clock! The geriatric nightlife starts earlier than most, I guess.

Turning off the engine, Seth grabs my gaze. "Wanna go outside?"

"Sure." Beats the ladies' room.

"That's a pretty dress, Scotty."

"Thanks. Grammie picked it out."

"She's really great." Of course, Seth won Grammie and Grampie over back at the RV. I don't think his politeness is an act. I've met his parents, remember?

"So what happened with Karissa?"

Seth helps me onto the hood of the truck and jumps up next

to me. Our feet dangle above the boat deck. "You were right. I hate to say it, not because I can't admit you've got insight that I don't, but . . . I guess I was just hoping that Karissa was who she was pretending to be."

"And who was that?"

"The beautiful girl with low self-esteem."

I bark out a laugh and he smiles.

"So tell me about it."

He leans back on his hands. "I asked her out for dinner to that place on Ocracoke, the one with the big watermelon on the sign."

"Yeah, I know it. The Flying Melon."

"So I got to the hotel a little early and went up to her room. I knocked and one of the twins answered, clearly drunk. It was, I don't know, six o'clock, I guess."

"She's what, thirteen?"

He blows a big spout of air through pursed lips. "So she swings the door really wide, and there's Karissa snorting coke off a mirror on the coffee table."

I don't say anything.

"Yeah, so, right. I see you're not at all shocked."

"Seth. Remember when you were in high school and you'd be invited over to a friend's house to watch a football game or something? Their parents weren't home and they'd be sipping on beer while they're yelling at the running backs to get a move on. Did that shock you?"

"That happened every weekend."

"My point exactly."

"It wasn't so much the shock of the drugs, Scotty. I've seen drugs before. It was that she swore she was clean and that it was all behind her now."

I lean back too. The stars are just starting to appear. "And Karissa *is* the beautiful girl with low self-esteem, Seth. The question is, are you strong enough to carry her baggage?"

"Shoot, I think sometimes I'm strong enough, but it's totally the wrong color suitcase, if you know what I'm saying."

"Some baggage we don't even want to try to tote along with us."

"It's like, *you've* definitely got baggage, but it's different."

"And we're just friends anyway," I say.

"True."

The burbling thrum of the ferry's motor shuffles the water behind us, and the moonlight jumps upon the inky path before us.

"So what happened after you caught her?"

"She looked up and saw me. I shook my head and said, 'No way,' and walked out of the room. She ran after me and before she could explain, I just told her forget it, consider it a set romance that never had a chance."

I giggle. "You said that? Sheesh, Seth, that sounds like a line from a made-for-TV movie."

"Tell me about it. But she had the last word. Some speech about how a nobody like me should have been thankful she even glanced my way."

"That's even more canned."

One side of his mouth lifts in a half smile. "You're a trip, Scotty."

I sit up straight and fold my feet yoga-style beneath my dress. "Well, I'm glad you came."

"Me too. You going to be okay, Scotty?"

"Yeah. Charley and me'll ride off into the sunset like always. This time, though, I'll know a little more, I guess. My real name is Ariana, Seth. Isn't that pretty?"

"Sure. But I like Scotty. It's sassy."

He smiles and leans forward. My heart stops, so does my breath. Will he? Oh it feels romantic here in the darkness. He tenderly takes my chin in his hand, pulls my face toward his, and I close my eyes as he kisses my forehead.

I want to cry. Here I thought I was doing so well, thinking of him as my big brother, but one false assumption and I'm nothing more than a gangly puppet, strings limp and disabled.

I face forward once again, willing my heart to slow down and my eyes to keep from tearing over. Thankfully it's too dark for him to see how blazing red my cheeks must be.

I clear my throat. "So what's happening with you then, after you leave?"

"I'm headed out to LA. I took a movie opposite Brad Pitt. I'm his son."

"You're kidding me. Brad Pitt with a teenage son?"

"Yeah. I guess he's finally admitting he's not the young guy he used to be."

I snort. "Hardly."

"Hey, I guess some people take longer than others to learn to see themselves for who they are."

"How are you going to live out there?"

"A friend of mine from college is trying to make it out there as a stand-up comic."

"No way!"

"Yeah. Anyway, we'll rent some dive somewhere together. We start shooting the film next month."

"Right in LA?"

"Yeah. Burbank. So that makes it nice."

I laugh and laugh and laugh. Burbank. Nice. Right.

"And where will you be going?" he asks.

"Who knows? Charley'll have something somewhere, and she won't tell me anything until the last minute."

"I'm sorry, Scotty."

"Yeah, well, Grampie had a good talk with me. Reamed me out in his nice way, to be honest. He told me I've got a great opportunity, living on the road like this, seeing what I get to see and how many other teenagers have a life like mine?"

"It's all how you decide to view it, I guess."

"So really—" I cross my arms—"do I have a bad attitude?"

He winces. "It's a little, well, acerbic. But Scotty, considering what your life's been like until now, I'd say you're doing pretty well."

But then again, Seth would say that, because Seth is a nice person.

Unlike Karissa Bonano.

"So when do you head out?" I ask as the boat chugs into the Ocracoke harbor.

"Tomorrow morning."

"Don't leave without saying good-bye." I almost choke out the words.

He puts his arm around me and squeezes. "I wouldn't think of doing anything that stupid."

Hollywood Nobody: April 25

Today's Total Scoop: Seth Haas and Karissa Bonano have called it quits. So much for anything serious. Looks like it was just a set romance after all. Well, we did think better of Seth, but our sources tell us he was the one who cooled off the steamy romance. Looks like he's got some sense inside that pretty head after all. I was beginning to wonder.

Today's Tidbit: Reese is seeing red! Well, we've seen her with blonde hair and brown hair, but until now we've never seen her with red hair. Check out Reese playing at the beach with her kids. I like it!

Today's Quote: "Hollywood is a place where they'll pay you a thousand dollars for a kiss and fifty cents for your soul." Marilyn Monroe

Check out Violette Dillinger's appearance on Letterman here on YouTube. I'd embed it, but . . .

It's late, Nobodies, and I'm pooped! But one quick parting note. Jeremy Winger's latest shoot has wrapped, and the cast and crew are getting out of Dodge. The people of Toledo Island are sure to be relieved their refuge will once again return to normal.

Later!

Comments:

good, I was getting sick of the whole thing. — Perezfan, 1:32 a.m.

Karissa can do better. — me_me_me, 2:05 a.m.

Monday, April 26

Wrapped in the comforter Grammie sent with me, I set aside the Bible Grampie bought me and slide open the window in my loft. Seth stands underneath, hands jammed in his pockets. "Hey, I'm going to leave in a little while. Want to take a walk on the beach?" It's five thirty in the morning.

"Sure."

I hop down from the bunk, swirl my hair into a clip, throw on jeans, sneakers, and the fisherman's sweater.

We're parked closer to the beach now, hidden behind some low-slung condo buildings. I inch the door open slowly so Charley won't hear and close it with just as much stealth.

"Ready?" He holds out his hand.

"Yeah." I put mine in his, grieving a little. He's a brother, nothing more. And he knows I know there will never be anything else, so he's comfortable now.

Yet it's good, really. Maybe I can be myself again, like that first night on the beach when we watched the little crabbies dance in the beam of the flashlight and skitter about sideways, lacking only top hats and canes.

"So, I'll miss you, Scotty."

"You scared about living in LA?"

"Hey, what guy is going to admit he's scared?"

"Okay, are you concerned?"

"Yeah."

We walk the path over the dune.

"Okay, I'm scared. I admit it."

"Well, you've got work, which is more than a lot of people

can say out there, so you're one step ahead of the game right at the start."

"True."

"And Brad Pitt? Come on! You're headed to the top if you give a good performance."

"You really think so?"

"Hey, I know a real star when I see one."

We stand in the slight glow of starlight and the ocean horizon beginning to lighten in anticipation of the rising sun.

"How will I get in touch with you?" he asks.

I squeeze his hand and let go. "Pretty much the same way you did here. I'll still have my cell phone."

"Oh. Yeah. I don't know why, but I feel like you're heading off into this thick fog and I won't be able to reach you."

"Funny, but I feel the same way about you, Seth. You have no idea what you're getting into. At least with me, I know what tomorrow will be like: another shoot, another director, another location to explore, some nice people to meet. It's always the same life at a different place. Still sneaking around, I'm sure."

"Charley needs to get a different RV if she wants to dodge this guy."

"That sure is the truth. But you're going to have to be really careful. We may be dodging somebody trying to hurt us. But you have to answer to yourself. As far as I'm concerned, that's when it really gets scary."

He bumps my shoulder with his. "How'd you get to be so smart?"

"Believe me, I've got a lot of time to think about stuff. And I've seen more examples of people making horrible choices than I can count, and at a very impressionable age too."

Seth shakes his head and laughs. "I'm really going to miss you. Promise me you'll keep in touch."

"I will. And there's e-mail too, you know."

"Okay. As soon as I get a computer set up, we can do that."

"And you can always contact me through Jeremy if all else fails."

We stand together, the surf pounding nearby.

Seth says, "Have you ever thought how each wave is just a little bit different as it smacks onto the shore?"

"And the beach it leaves behind as it goes out isn't quite the same ever again, is it?"

"No, Scotty. It isn't. It never is."

Seth puts his arms around me; I hug him around the waist and lay my head on his chest. The sun will rise and we'll go our separate ways, but it will be the same sun shining on us both. For now, I guess I'll rest in that.

Later

Jeremy opens the door of his Airstream, and right away we smell his beef stew. He always makes a beef stew at the end of a shoot, chunks of chuck roast dredged in flour, salt, and pepper, then browned in olive oil. Butter, carrots, golden potatoes, pearl onions and peas soak up the gravy. "Hey, kiddo. Come on in, Charley. Don't worry, I made a salad too."

"Can I have some stew, Charley?" I ask.

"Sure, baby."

Seems like the woman is coming around in some ways, you know?

I've been anticipating this all day. One half of me very sad about Seth's departure, the other half stretched with anxiousness over "the talk." Charley needs Jeremy for support, so it must be big. Plus Jeremy's a better storyteller than Charley, so I have this feeling he'll be doing all the talking. It's okay.

Charley pours some bottled water in glasses and sets out napkins. She really knows her way around Jeremy's trailer.

I slide into the dinette at the back. It's so space-age and vintage in an Airstream.

Jeremy's trying to act relaxed and loose like always, but I'm not buying it because he's drinking decaf coffee, and Jeremy never drinks decaf unless he's upset. He dishes up stew. Heavenly. Then pulls some garlic bread out of the oven.

We sit down and start to eat.

"Jeremy, you did it perfectly. Again."

He winks.

"Good salad, Jere," Charley says.

He winks at Charley.

I bite into the garlic bread. Lots of butter, lots of garlic, lots of basil, and lots of Parmesan. Go, Jeremy. "So who's gonna start this rap session?" I figure I'll use their vernacular.

Charley looks at Jeremy. "Why don't you go ahead."

Jeremy sets his big spoon inside his bowl, chews up the bite, swallows, and wipes his mouth. "It's like this, Scotty. Your real name is Ariana, like you guessed. And Charley's real name isn't Charley."

"Really?"

Charley nods. "It's been my nickname ever since the commune days, but my name is actually Regina."

"That's a pretty name," I say. "Regina and Ariana. Wow. That sure is different from Charley and Scotty."

"Exactly." Jeremy picks up his napkin. "So here's the story, kid. When you were born, you and your mother lived in Baltimore. When Charley had to change your names, she chose the name of your — a relative's favorite author, F. Scott Fitzgerald. Dawn is just a last name she chose."

I turn to Charley. She has tears in her eyes. "What was my last name before that?"

She just looks at her hands. "I'm not saying, Scotty. It's for your own good."

Jeremy clears his throat. "Yeah, so anyway. Your mother was involved with a real rich guy at that time."

"My father?"

"Right. He married her, moved her into a ritzy home in Mt. Vernon, went to work every day, traveled sometimes like businessmen do, but she never really knew what he actually did. I mean, she thought she knew, but the truth was very different."

Charley nods.

"So one day, guess what? Your mother follows him, because she forgets to tell him about a dinner party they're going to that night. He walks down the street, quite a few blocks, and for some reason, she doesn't call out. She gets one of those weird feelings to just keep walking without saying anything. You know how it goes sometimes?"

"Yes. You can't explain it, but you know something's not quite right."

"Exactly." He looks up at Charley. "She was suspecting he was having an affair, him being gone a lot and not really saying where he was. So they go down by the waterfront, quite a hike, over in Canton before it was all redone so upscale, and he disappears into this warehouse."

"Used to be a bakery," Charley whispers.

"And so your mother follows him in there and she gets inside and she sees some men standing around. To make a long story short, one of them was a gubernatorial candidate, hand in hand with the mob. She recognized the mobster because she was a journalist—"

"You were a journalist?"

"Just listen, baby."

"Yeah, big stuff. Your father was standing there and one of the heavyweights turns on your father, says something about how he knows he's undercover with the FBI and shoots him in the chest."

I feel like he's slapped me across the face. He should have warned me. I try to breathe.

"Charley, is this is a good idea?"

I gulp in air. My father. My father. My cheese-loving father. "I want to know. Please."

My father's dead! My father's dead. I was so sure.

Oh, you stupid idiot, Scotty.

"Your mom wasn't stupid, she sees what's going on, knows it must have something to do with buying the election. It was that big. She gasps and runs from the building."

"Where was I?"

"With your grandmother."

"That was good."

"Right."

"Who's my grandmother?"

I don't know how much more I can handle. Did I say I wanted to know that truth? How naïve!

"Let me finish this part. Unfortunately we don't have all the details and can only fill in the gaps. She hides in the back of a friend's gallery until she's sure they're all gone, and then runs to your grandmother's place and says for her to keep you with her for a while. Until she sees what's going on. You can imagine the emotional pain she was in."

Charley lays her hands flat on the table. "Stop, Jeremy."

Jeremy takes off his glasses, rubs down his face with a sideways hand. "Okay, then. Just trying to help."

She places a hand over his. "I know. I appreciate it."

This is totally crazy. "You all are totally crazy."

"I know." Charley pushes her salad away from her. "Okay, what you've heard is true, Scotty, minus one little detail. I'm not your mother. I'm your grandmother."

"What?!"

"I'm sorry, Scotty. I'm not your mother."

First my dad. Now . . . oh, my gosh. Oh no.

The trailer shrinks in that moment, so hot. I slip off the seat and run for the water. The lies were bigger and grander than I thought. No mother. No mother. A dead father. Charley's not my mother. The frigid, orphan waves receive me. So cold. So cold.

"Scotty!" Charley screams from shore. "Oh, Scotty!"

A breaker crashes into me, slamming me under it. So cold.

Dear Elaine,

So this is how it all went down: After my real mother (my gosh, I'm still reeling, like falling-down-and-unable-to-breathe upset), Babette, Babette is her name, dropped me off at Charley's, she disappeared. Charley took me back to Babette's house several days later as they'd arranged, and the place was empty. The next-door neighbor said that some guys had come with a moving truck, packed up everything and left. What about the woman? Charley asked.

The men said she was killed in a car accident.

Charley knew Babette, my mom, would get in touch with her if she was alive, but after several months she realized her daughter must have been killed—and probably not in a car accident. Babette, my mom, was apparently really, really devoted to me.

Somehow the mob pieced together that Charley knew what was going on. Nobody knows how—bugging the phone, Charley's house, I don't know. Powerful people get information, and that's the bottom line. We just don't know. But they tried to kill us one night by setting our house on fire. We just barely escaped. Charley told the neighbors that if anybody came poking around, they should say we were dead.

I'm telling you, Elaine, this is awful. So Charley hit the road in the Y and for the past thirteen years has eluded everyone. Until now. That dirty governor is running for president now, and Charley is especially frightened. And Biker Guy is coming around, and she knows that we are found and it's only a matter of time.

Am I scared? Totally. Totally. Totally.

The day I found out I have a real mother whose name is Babette, I found out she is dead. The day I found out about my father, an undercover federal agent, I found out he died a hero's death.

And Charley. She's so brave. I have bravery running through me. Though my sadness is deep, there's something to cling to, something strong and good.

Tuesday, April 27

I hug Joy, drink one last cup of her coffee, and tell her how great I think she is.

"I've decided to go back to New York," she says. "I'm going to design for plus-size women. And I'm going to never be a size two again. Healthy and happy."

"That's great!"

"Yep." She sweeps a hand around the diner. "I'm going to miss this place, though."

"I'll bet. They'll miss you too."

Her eyes fill with tears. "Benjamin will be with me wherever I go. It's not like I'm leaving his memory behind."

"No. Not even close."

She crosses her fingers. "So . . . I guess we're both heading in new directions."

"Will you send me something from your first collection?"

"I'll have to size it down, but you got it. I don't know what I would have done without you, Scotty."

She kisses me on the cheek.

"So how about a piece of your key-lime pie for the road?"

"A piece? Honey-girl, you can have the entire pie!"

Saturday, May 1

And so, four days later, as Charley and I pull the Y into Delightful Days RVs, I'm thinking about how I can't forget to transfer the remaining half of pie into the new RV.

Well, new to us.

We walk around the lot and wonder if getting a fifth wheel and a big pickup wouldn't be a better option.

"Then how will we trail the kitchen trailer?" I ask. "And we can't lie around in back if the other one is driving. Nah, I think we really need to keep it a class C—I'll take the loft and you take the bed in the back. Just like always."

"You sure?"

"Positive. Can we just not paint a rainbow on this one, Charley?"

"You got it. Besides, we've got to blend in now. You know?"

"And that rainbow is pretty much a neon sign."

"It is. I don't know what I was thinking. I was just hoping it was all over. That we were forgotten. I'd left so much of myself behind . . . I just thought with the rainbow . . ."

Wow. Maybe I should start trying to see things through Charley's eyes a little bit, give her some credit. She lost her daughter and her son-in-law and has done the best she can to raise their child. No wonder she's so sad. I mean, no wonder.

I link my arm through hers and we saunter around the lot. Wow, these things are nice these days, aren't they? We might not be able to afford a Beaver Marquis or anything, but I'm not going to complain right now. It's something new, and we'll do just fine.

At least for a little while.

"Oh, look!" Charley points to a dark blue Trailmaster. "What do you think of that one?"

"Let's take a look."

When we step up into the tan-toned interior, homey and smelling clean and nice, I realize that we've found a new home. Me and Charley, my grandmother.

"Charley, I love you."

"I love you too, baby. I'm so sorry about all of this, this life, these secrets."

She puts her arms around me and holds me close.

I lift my head. "It's okay. So long as you don't try to control every move I make anymore, Charley. I think we've got to learn to take chances here and there. And maybe trust God to protect us."

From what I've been reading in the book of Acts lately, apostles sprung from prison cells and whatnot, so that's not such a farfetched thought.

"Yeah," she whispers. "That's a hard thing for me to do after all that's happened."

"Hey, we've been safe so far."

She smiles. "Well, yeah. We have been. There's definitely that."

"And we need to renegotiate my diet. In a month I'll be sixteen. I think I can decide what I can and cannot eat."

"Oh, Scotty. Not now. I mean, we've just been through so much and you're going to bring up cheese, aren't you?"

"Of course. Charley, I don't want cheese to be wrong. You're making it like some sort of sin or something. I'm old enough to decide that cheese is definitely okay."

She rolls her eyes and pulls me into a tight hug. "Oh, all right! Cheese it is. Eat it all you like. I give up."

"Thanks." I'm loving this. I'm not gonna lie.

We inspect the little bathroom. Separate shower/tub. Nice.

I turn to Charley. "I can live here. How about you?"

"Yes, baby. I can too."

And somehow, we both realize we're talking about more than this RV. A whole lot more.

Hollywood Nobody: May 2

Sorry it's been a few days, Nobodies, but we've been busy changing locations. Where? You'll never know, but this one's coming to you from the road!

Today's Quote: "I'm very glad I'm a normal-sized person, and I shall continue to be a normal-sized person, enjoying my food." Kate Winslet

Speaking of enjoying food. Remember that fabulous designer Joy Overstreet, who disappeared a few years ago? Look for her designs again soon, for plus-size, or as I like to say, *curvy* women everywhere.

Seth Watch: The hottie is moving to LA to star alongside Brad Pitt. As his teenage son! Whoa, Brad, gettin' a little old there, aren't we? I love it. I'm not gonna lie.

Today's Rant: Honestly? I'm in a good place today. No rants. But just give me until tomorrow!

Later!

Comments:

Hollywood Nobody, if you're reading this, hop on IM! I've got exciting news and want you to have the scoop! You're not going to believe this! — Violette, 4:32 p.m.

AVAILABLE MARCH 2008

lisa samson

Finding
Hollywood
Nobody

a novel

Sample from

Finding Hollywood Nobody

I head over to Ms. Burrell's, the costume mistress's trailer. She's pushing fabric so fast through her industrial machine I have to shut my mouth. I know enough about Ms. Burrell — feisty, assured, and the color of cocoa powder — to wait until she looks up at me.

After a minute she does. "Well, Scotty, my baby! Come here and give me hug."

Mmm. Ms. Burrell's figure could be described as "heroic." All I know is I love to be enfolded in her big warm arms. She smells like coconut, a description that matches her hair, bleached and lying in short, cream-colored quills around her head.

I pull back. "Karissa Bonano."

"Baby, I *know*! I said to Jeremy, 'That sweat box? Again?!' And of course, he just laughed. This is a gothic piece, Scotty, a gothic horror piece about . . . you read the script yet?"

"No. I think Charley hides them from me because she knows how mad they always make me."

"Well, I know. But this one is actually pretty good. It's about this girl lost in an old hotel, and she goes crazy because all around her are the excesses of life and, baby, she's going to try it all."

I open a nearby folding chair and set it up next to her worktable. "So what's the hitch?"

"With each thing she tries, she loses a little bit of herself."

"Like, literally?"

"Uh-huh. Wakes up one morning without a pinkie and so forth from then on out."

"Ewww!"

"You got that right."

"She must be pretty stupid."

"Which is why Jeremy got Karissa Bonano — ha haaaah!"

True 'dat. Or whatever it is people who are a lot cooler than I am say. I'm not good at cool-speak. Not even close. I prefer to think of myself as "the intelligent type above all that."

My cell phone buzzes.

Ms. Burrell rolls her liquid brown eyes. "Oh, go ahead. You all and your phones!"

A text. Oh, cool. Sue me, but I love text messaging.

It's from Seth!

Where are u?

In Texas.

Why?

Jeremy's pet project. Where are you?

Going 2 the set. brd pitt awaits. ha!

Is he nice?

Yeah. Lks a lot oldr in prson.

I'll bet. How much longer on the set?

A few days, thn we go on lcation to vermnt.

Cool.

I may stp by tx on the way. ill hve a few days off.

Very cool. Let me know when.

Ok. cu!

Backatcha.

I shut my phone. Seth is a very minimalist text messager. And I don't think he knows how to work the shift key for capital letters, but that's okay.

"So who was that?" Ms. Burrell reaches behind her and grabs a bolt of lavender chiffon.

"Seth Haas."

"Oh, I love that boy. How's he doing?"

"Fine. Is playing alongside Brad Pitt."

"No!"

"Yes."

"I'm not surprised. I been around these parts for a long time and I know whose got it, and that boy's got it."

"If he can stay away from Karissa Bonano. He's coming to visit for a couple of days. She'll be here. You know what I'm saying?"

She shakes her head. "I've seen young men do stupider things." She leans forward and whispers, "You think she'll get him in her clutches again?"

The hair on the back of my neck stands up. "No. He's smarter than that, right?"

And Ms. Burrell laughs and laughs.

It's time to get going on this year's schoolwork. I took the summer off completely, lounged around online with my blog and the other Hollywood rags, ate a lot of cheese, and actually found a few online courses that will extend me credit and a diploma. I'm pretty behind in "real" classes, but give me two years and I'll have all the minimum requirements.

However, seeing as we travel from place to place, I consider myself a traveling historian. During the drive here yesterday, I checked out Marshall and figure the best place to begin is The

Ginocchio Hotel, which I picture like Pinocchio, a long skinny nose somehow protruding from its side like a huge flagpole.

Anyway.

I grab my scooter, a little Razor-esque job with a motor and a seat, buzz out to Washington Street and take a left moving southward. Just shy of the hotel, a teenager stalks up the cement steps of an old stone house. She falls. Her cry sends me up to the curb and I jump off the scooter, fling my backpack down, and hurry up the steps to where she sits.

She looks up at me, tears and anger streaking her made-up face. She's pretty in a sad, wistful way, rounded cheeks and deep blue eyes that pare the sunlight to a minimum with a squint. "I knew I was taking those too fast. Darn it, I'm so clumsy!"

"It's okay." I sit down on the steps just below her. "These old steps can be so steep, and people were shorter back then than they are now. It makes no sense whatsoever. But it is what it is, right? And are you okay?"

Man, I'm chattering like a monkey!

"Yeah." She pulls up the right leg of her jeans. A bleeding sidewalk burn.

"Ouch."

"Yeah," she nods. "It stings."

Her Texas accent makes two syllables out of one and she manages a slanty smile.

"Here, I've got some antibiotic ointment in my backpack."

Yes, I'm the nerdiest of all nerds.

"It's not one of those alcohol kinds, is it?"

"Nope."

She leans back in relief. "Thanks. My name is Grace, by the way."

"I'm Scotty."

"Do you go to Marshall High?"

"Nah. I'm here with the film shoot."

"Wow. Really?"

"Uh-huh." I tell her about Charley the TrailMama, road school, my basic, ridiculous life, as I pat on the ointment. "I don't have a bandage."

I'm not that much of a nerd.

"It's okay, I'm headed inside anyway."

You know, every once in a while, you're pulled from your current reality by the realization that something new and improved is happening. Like now. I'm sitting here on a cement stoop in a small Texas town having a real-life conversation with a girl my age. A girl that goes to a real-life high school.

"How old are you?" I ask.

"Sixteen."

"Me too!"

"Cool." So she's not as excited about that fact as I am, and why would she be?

"So I hope you feel better. You live here?"

She jumps up. "No! I was just peeking in to have a look. They've been trying to rent the place out for months. It's empty."

"Oh."

Maybe teenagers have a habit of looking into deserted houses clearly marked No Trespassing. I mean, what do I know? I want to ask her a thousand questions, but my tongue sits like an anvil in my mouth and despite my deep desire, I cannot.

I stand up too. "Well, I'd better get down to the museum. I'm doing research for history."

"Good luck on that. Sounds cool."

"Thanks. Maybe I'll see you around."

"Maybe, but I live on the other side of town. So see ya."

"Okay."

Once down the steps, I hop on my scooter and finish descending the hill. Hotel Ginocchio here I come.

Securing my scooter to a nearby light pole, and thank goodness for light poles, I look up the street. Grace is gone.

I only half listen as the tour guide shares details about the hotel with me, and I know I'll have to come back soon and hear it all over again. But I do take note of the part about how the manager, seated in his office on the second floor, had a clear shot down to the safe behind the desk on the first.

Were things different back then or what?

I can't keep my mind on my studies. I mean, really, would one more day hurt? Doesn't reading F. Scott Fitzgerald count?

I would say yes.

And what better place to read than a coffee shop? I sail back up the street to Jacob and Luke's Coffee. It's the cutest place, a squat, white Victorian home (and yeah, this town is totally back in time) with a circular porch to the right of the green front door.

"Excuse me," an elderly lady says, smiling as she exits.

I step to the side as a parade of women follow, the same novel tucked under a few arms, and wouldn't it be fun to be a part of a book club? Charley and I are never in the same place long enough for those kinds of activities.

Inside the funky room, done up in shades of gold and green and even turquoise, corrugated tin, and scratchy old wood, I order a whole-milk latte and try to decide which "smash"—

panini sandwich — to order. Yeah, very cute. The spirit of Charley whispers, "Order the veggie smash, order the veggie smash." I flick her out of the way like an annoying fly.

"I'll take Jacob's Reuben Smash."

The man behind the counter nods and punches a button on the cash register. "It's my favorite. But I made one slight change."

I lean forward and whisper. "Are you Jacob then?"

He nods, winks. "But don't let on."

We laugh out loud.

"So what's the change?"

"You tell me after you've taken a bite."

"Deal."

He hands me my receipt and says, "Jeanne will bring it to the table when it's ready."

Jeanne sets down my latte. She is beautiful, an almost dead ringer for Kirsten Scott Thomas. Short, with sandy-blonde hair and one of those assured attitudes every woman hopes she has. At least I imagine they do. I sure do, anyway. Smiley eyes. Really pretty and a prime example of why Hollywood women have it so wrong to go so plastic — her laugh lines make me want to laugh too. "Here you go, sweetie. Sandwich will be right up."

I head up the steps to the left of the coffee bar and into what must have once been a sun porch. Windows line the room. I choose one of two totally vintage, totally cool, green Naugahyde chairs, each chair back bull's-eyed with a three-inch wide, fabulous button. You just gotta love those crazy fifties designers, don't you? I set my latte on the rattan ottoman, pull out *Tender Is the Night*, and steep myself in the languor of summer on the French Riviera.

I hear a commotion down on the main floor. And so I am pulled out of warm sands and rich people, some certifiably crazy and others just silly, lying around in the sun, leaving me to wonder where on earth they got all that money in the first place!

Jeanne's head appears in the stairwell, then her neck, chest, waist, and finally the rest of her as she climbs the steps. "Here we go. Jacob's famous Reuben."

"So what's the difference?"

She sets the sandwich on the ottoman. "I'll give you a hint. It's about the cheese."

"Oh, I'm all about the cheese!"

"Then you'll guess it right away." She crosses her arms. "Go ahead. Take a bite."

I do, crunching through the fresh, grilled rye bread, my teeth slicing through Russian dressing, sauerkraut, cheese, and layers of moist corned beef and oh, my goodness, does Charley really know what she's missing?

I start to really taste the ingredients, closing my eyes to segment the tastes, particularly the cheese. Oh, yes. It's clear, so very clear.

I open my eyes. "I got it."

"Well?"

"He used provolone."

She smacks one hand down onto the leg of her blue jeans. "Yes! That's it. Good job." She cocks her head toward the stairwell and the increasing commotion.

"What's going on down there?"

"I think it's a famous actress. From the film shoot. You heard about the film shoot?"

I explain.

"Oh." She crosses her arms. "Well, then maybe you can tell me who this gal is. Acts like she's running the world in that Paris Hilton sort of way."

"Blonde and skinny?" Which describes seventy-five percent of Hollywood.

"But with a big chest that doesn't match the rest of her."

"Yes. That's Karissa Bonano." She must have had plastic surgery on her chest while she was in rehab.

Jeanne throws her weight on one leg. "I must be out of touch. I've never heard of her."

"She's been around forever."

"How old is she?"

"Nineteen."

Jeanne throws out a full-on laugh. "Nineteen? She's old enough to be my child. Believe me, that is not forever ago! You know her?"

"Yeah. Kinda."

"Want me to tell her you're up here?"

"No way. Please, please, please don't do that!"

A few minutes later, The Karissa materializes in much the same manner Jeanne did. I raise my book to hide my face.

She's by herself. Nobody follows.

Well, this is Marshall, Texas. I doubt people get excited about a Hollywood teen queen beyond the shock of first sight.

Her phone rings and I prepare myself to shamelessly eavesdrop, which means I poke my nose even farther into the pages of my book.

"It's Karissa. Hey, Linds."

Lindsay Lohan? Maybe.

"No, I'm here already. This town is about as exciting as Early

American furniture."

Okay, I didn't think her capable of that kind of metaphor.

"What are you up to?"

Probably rehab.

"You saw him? On the lot? How'd he look?"

Who's *he*?

"They cut his curls off for the role? That's terrible. How does it look?"

What curls?

I pull out my laptop, hop online, Google Seth Haas, and find the latest picture of him, head shorn close. No! No way! She cannot possibly still be interested in him.

But yes, he's still cute.

"So what did he say?"

That he never wants to see you again, you lying wench, catching you with cocaine at the last shoot. What do you expect him to say?

"Well, that's encouraging. Sort of, you know?"

It better not be. I'm so texting Seth as soon as I get away from KB and her phone friend.

"I gotta go. I've got lines to learn for tomorrow and I found a quiet spot in a coffee shop. Just some bookworm here in the room with me." She whispers that last line.

Well, I've got to hand it to her, at least she knows a book when she sees one.

I'm just sayin'.

About the Author

LISA SAMSON is the author of twenty books, including the Christy Award-winning *Songbird*. *Hollywood Nobody* is her first Young Adult book. She speaks at various writers' conferences throughout the year. Lisa and her husband, Will, reside in Kentucky with their three children. Learn more about Lisa at www.hollywoodnobody.com.